The Yard Sale of Life

The 8 Coats of Meaning

Straight Talk from Spirit
Book II

Carol Gino

Published by aaha! Books
New York & Texas
www.aahabooks.com
www.rashanasgarden.com

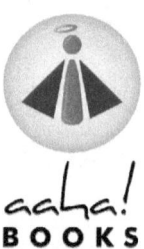

BOOKS

ISBN-10: 193653018X
EAN-13: 9781936530182

Library of Congress Control Number: 2014917278
aaha! Books, LLC, Smithville, TX

EPub-978-1-936530-19-9
Kindle-978-1-936530-20-5

Dedicated to all those who believe in the
magic of Dreams
and trust their inner Guidance

Other books by Carol Gino
The Nurse's Story
Rusty's Story
Then An Angel Came
The Family by Mario Puzo—Completed
by Carol Gino
There's An Angel In My Computer
Where Dreams Come True
The Azurite

Author's Note

It's been said that a civilization that has lost its stories has lost its way. Today it isn't easy to see our planet's future through reality's eyes. And though imagination has been devalued with the rise of the rational, it isn't hard to see that the key to our planet's future rests on our ability to imagine it. Science has proven that all great discoveries begin by imagining them.

New pathways in our brain must be created and traveled in order for each of us to evolve. Without imagination, there are no dreams; without dreams, there is no future, only a constantly repeating present without magic.

Our minds create concepts, but our souls create myth. The images of our imagination must reach to the depths of our soul to renegotiate the contract in our souls' DNA in order to translate our dreams and transform our lives. That can be done—it is possible—but not with thought alone. New territory must be explored and developed, and only imagination and story can take us there.

There are no illustrations in this book on purpose. Rashana's hope, and mine, is that as you take this journey with us, you can travel your own path and begin to carve new pathways in your own brain. For it is a simple truth that this is the only way to create a richer and fuller life in the present.

With great hope and love, we offer these truths to you.

Carol Rashana

Intro to the Yardsale

Chapter 1
The Yardsale

It was a bright, shiny morning and the sun was peeking through my plantation shutters trying to nudge me into waking. I was feeling really lazy, and in no rush to jump up and start my day.

But I know I wasn't dreaming. I was lying in bed, caught in that place between sleeping and waking as a movie played on the inner screen of my mind.

Suddenly, she was there again.

Rashana, who claims to be my spirit of joy and creativity, and the answer to all those prayers I sent to the heavens for a Divine vision. She was wearing a pink angel costume. Wrinkled. She says she dresses up like a virtually perfect angel to please me because I feel safe and comfortable with angels. Her blond hair hung loosely over her shoulders. That morning she was wearing pink ballet slippers and prancing up and down in front of me doing her usual cloud dance.

"Want to go to the Yardsale?" she asked sweetly.

"Sure," I said, "I've never been to one."

I know that surprised her, because I'm usually moaning and groaning about all the work I have to do, all the pages I can't write, or all the money I'll not have unless I get to work. I'm a writer, and I need to write pages in order to finish my books.

She always tells me I'm out of balance and that what I really need to learn to do, is play. Then it will all work out. It's clear to me she's from another realm and doesn't have to pay rent and bills or buy food.

Anyway, I agreed to go with her because I truly had never been to a yardsale. Rashana didn't care why I agreed; she was just tickled that I was finally willing to play.

Suddenly, like in those animated movies, there was a scene change and I was standing in front of what looked like a huge Yardsale. Out of nowhere, I saw a guy leaning against the gate of a white picket fence. He looked like an aging hippie, with curly gray hair sticking out all over his head, faded jeans, and a red-and-black flannel shirt. Around his neck, he wore a long string of multi-colored love beads and a sterling-silver peace sign pendant. As we approached, he flashed me a really great smile—a toothpaste-white smile—and said, "Howdy."

I smiled back and waved as we walked toward him. Rashana was silently standing next to me. "Is this your Yardsale?" I asked the man when we got close enough.

He looked at me with a half-amused expression and winked at Rashana when he repeated, "*My* Yardsale?" Then he chuckled and added, "Nope. Not my Yardsale."

"Whose is it then?" I asked.

He raised his eyebrows and said, "I guess you could say it belongs to everyone, sort of like a Cosmic Yardsale."

I frowned, figuring he was on drugs or something, but Rashana was giggling having a really good time.

"Maybe I'll just look around," I said to both of them.

The hippie held out his hand to shake mine. "Name's Pete," he said.

"Mine's Carol," I told him. I turned to Rashana to introduce her to Pete, but I saw her smile at him, so I knew there was no need.

Then Pete asked us, "Got karma cash or karmic credit?"

I didn't have a clue what he was talking about, but Rashana answered, "She's got both. She's had a savings account in the Universal Bank of One for lifetimes and enough debt for interest."

I turned to Rashana. "What are you talking about?" I asked. Then I reached into my pocket but it was empty. "Where's my money? I always carry a couple of dollars with me."

Both Rashana and Pete looked at me with puzzled expressions. "You can't use money," Rashana said. "It's false currency. You need a different kind of currency here."

"Different currency?" I asked. "What kind?"

"It has to be universal, and it has to be real," Rashana said.

Pete interrupted. "Here we accept any currency based on growth, choice, and personal responsibility. We accept both cash and credit on the universal exchange."

Rashana turned to Pete and handed him some kind of a card. "Use this account," she said. "There's enough there to get Soulee whatever she wants."

"Thanks," he said, and then he turned toward me. "What ya looking for?" he asked. He had a slow, drawn-out way of speaking—a kind of drawl.

Rashana started to walk around ahead of us, looking over the long, littered tables; picking stuff up; and staring at it for long minutes. Then, as she kept walking, I saw her peeking into several colorful tents, curiously absorbed in everything as she wandered farther and farther away from me. I tried to keep my eyes on her, but suddenly she seemed to disappear.

I focused my attention back on Pete. "I'm not looking for anything in particular," I told him. "I've just never been to a yard sale before."

"It's a big one," he said. "Lots of sections. Nothing special you want?"

"Not really," I said. I was embarrassed to admit that I had no idea what was being offered.

Pete seemed to sense my confusion. "You want to pick a direction and just start walking, or what?"

The grass was vibrant green and lush, and all manner of things were scattered across it, some on tables, some freestanding, and some in big tents. There were lots of people roaming around.

"I don't know," I said. "I haven't any idea where to begin."

I looked toward Rashana for direction, but she just waved to me from far across the yard.

"I can take you to my favorite spot," Pete offered. He seemed like a nice guy, and he wasn't the least bit pushy.

"Are you a guide or something?" I asked as we began to walk.

He looked down at the ground, shuffled his feet a little, and said humbly, "I'm just watching over the place."

I smiled again. "OK," I said. "You mean you're the caretaker. I can understand why you'd like this kind of job. You have freedom, and you can work outside instead of in one of those corporate cubicles. Not bad. Take me wherever you want to go."

Pete kept walking, and I followed him. Occasionally I saw something that glittered and glistened on one of the tables, but nothing really caught my attention enough to stop me. Finally, after walking for what seemed like a long time, Pete stopped and held out his arms as though presenting a beautiful landscape.

"Well, here we are!" he announced gaily.

"Toasters?" I said, surprised. Truly, for what seemed like miles, all I could see were toasters—old ones, shiny ones, dull ones, even some new toaster ovens, but still, only toasters. I looked at Pete for an explanation.

"I *love* toasters," Pete said. "Want one?"

I shook my head. "No," I said. "Thank you. I have a toaster."

"It works great?" he asked. "Makes golden-brown toast every time?"

"Pretty much," I said, not understanding his fascination with toasters.

"You know how they work?" he asked.

"Yes. You plug them into the outlet, push down the button, and soon the electricity heats up the coils and toasts your bread," I said.

"Right!" he said. "Amazing, huh?"

"Not really," I said. "It's just how a toaster works."

Pete looked at me and smiled, his large blue eyes sparkling with happiness. "It doesn't excite you? That it fulfills its promise, does just what it says it will do? You don't want to choose another?"

"Pete," I said apologetically but with a slight bit of annoyance, "I have a toaster. I know how it works. It's a good toaster, and I don't need another."

Pete shook his head. "Looks like you've finished the toaster experience. Looks like you're done with it." He shrugged his shoulders and with a deep sigh and a soft voice said, "God, I sure love toasters." Then he looked at me hopefully and asked, "You think I could write a book on the nature of toasters, their integrity and single-focused perfection?"

It would have to be a booklet, I thought, but what I said was, "I don't know, Pete; I really don't know."

Pete saw I was getting impatient. "You want to go on, right?"

I nodded. I looked around for Rashana, but she seemed to be gone, wandering around the Yardsale still looking at stuff herself.

"OK," Pete said, trying to sound cheery. "I'll take you somewhere else." But in his blue eyes, I glimpsed a hint of sadness.

After what seemed like another very long walk across more and more lush green grass dotted with all kinds of used junk and vintage treasures, we arrived at a place that reminded me of an oil painting by Pieter Brueghel the Elder. It was a very crowded painting. Bunches of adults with their heads covered in white skullcaps, sprouted from windows in old attached brick houses. The women were hanging clothes that were blowing in the wind on sagging clotheslines. Little children on the ground looked up at other children hanging from rooftops dumping buckets of water on the people below. All were dressed in warm medieval browns and oranges. There were people all over the place, some clustered in groups and some separate, standing alone in corners. It was a very rich but confusing scene.

"This is our Family section," Pete announced proudly.

"A Family section?" I asked. "I don't get it."

"You want a family?" he said. "You can just walk in and be a part of one, or you can take one home if you like."

This is pretty weird, I thought, but all I said was, "I have a family."

"What kind of family?" Pete asked with real interest. "A good one?"

I smiled at him. "A good family. A big family. An Italian family," I said. "I don't need another family. In fact, the one thing I'm sure of is that I don't want another family."

Pete nodded his head in understanding. Then he held his chin, and his eyes got a faraway look. He seemed thoughtful. "We have other kinds of families here. We have bad families. Dysfunctional families. Small families," he told me.

"No," I said. "I don't *want* another family. My family is fine. I like my family, and honestly, I'm not interested in more families."

Pete took a deep breath and said under his breath, just loud enough for me to hear, "I thought everyone wanted a family. So what do I know?"

"Where can we go next?" I asked him.

"Well, right up ahead a few miles, there's another section you'll really like," he said with confidence. "Almost everyone likes this section."

"Miles?" I said.

"Just an expression," he said. "Could've said 'years' or 'frequency.' It's just an expression."

Drugs, I thought. It must be drugs.

Suddenly, ahead of us, there appeared a deep, green vale. Surrounding it, the small hills were covered with bright wildflowers of yellow and blue and tall trees with green leaves swaying in a gentle breeze. As I turned my head a bit, I saw what looked like a gray and stormy sky. There were people here too—a mother holding a crying child, two lovers holding hands, an older couple sitting together on a park bench.

"What's this section?" I asked.

"Relationships," he said. Pete smiled as though he had finally come upon something.

But I frowned. "I have a relationship," I said.

He had been standing a little in front of me, and now he turned his head to look at me, surprised. "You have a relationship?" he asked. "A good one?"

I nodded. "A good one," I said. "A fine and loving one," I added firmly, thinking I'd put the discussion to rest and we could move on.

"You want to try a bad one?" he asked seriously. "We have lots of different kinds here. Loving, but you said you had that. We also have broken relationships, abusive relationships, passionate relationships...."

"Stop," I said, holding up my hand. "I have a relationship. It's enough. I don't want another."

Pete scratched his head and looked puzzled. Then he just slowly folded his legs and sat down on the grass like a yogi. When he picked up a long blade of grass and ran it across his upper lip, I frowned. "I'm thinking," he explained in response to my quizzical expression. But he looked as though he'd be thinking for quite a while, so I dropped down onto the grass alongside him. "OK," he said. "Let's see if I can get this straight. You have a toaster, you have a family, and you have a relationship, right?"

"Right," I said. "And I don't want any more of those things."

Pete looked confused.

"Maybe there's nothing here that I want," I said, trying to take the pressure off him.

"Maybe," he said. "But you haven't begun to look at most of it yet. We probably just haven't hit on it. You got no ideas? Still no direction you want to go?"

I shook my head and shrugged my shoulders.

Pete fell backward in what looked like slow motion. He lay down on the grass and stared at the blue, cloudless sky.

"You happy?" he asked softly.

"Pretty much," I said.

"When you're *not* happy," he asked, "what's that about? What do you want then?"

I thought about it. "I don't always know," I said.

"Hmm…" he said, but that was all. After a few more moments of silence, he began to reminisce. "You know, you got to be careful about judging what's important to people. Some people's toss-aways is other people's treasures. There's no telling how important anything is."

"I know you're trying to tell me something, Pete," I said. "But I'm afraid I'm not getting it."

"Well, I was just thinking about somebody I came across a little while ago."

He seemed troubled so I asked, "Would it help to talk about it?"

"It's just that I know it's not my business to make judgments for other people, but sometimes my mind just does it automatically. Some thought in me just jumps up front and thinks it knows what's really important for someone else. Some dictator aspect in me."

"We all do that sometimes," I said, "Don't be so hard on yourself."

Pete shook his head. "I don't like to hurt people's feelings," he admitted. "And this time I'm afraid I did. I was a little too smug, even a bit condescending."

"It happens," I said.

He looked over at me, sizing me up, and then I guess he decided I might understand, so he began to tell me his story.

He started slowly, his eyes searching within. "There was a woman, a frail little thing, who came up to the entrance of the yard sale the other morning," he said, remembering. "She asked me for a bottle, a cobalt-blue bottle. In fact, she even pulled out a picture she had drawn of it. When she talked about it, she was so excited that both her hands and her voice were shaking, and I wondered what could be so important about a blue bottle. And, if it was so important, why was she so particular about its shape, dimensions, and even its color?"

Pete took a deep breath and swallowed hard, as though he found it painful to talk about. Then he said, "I must have said something like, 'Hey, lady, what's so important about a blue bottle? It's only a bottle.' I guess my voice gave me away. Well, this poor little thing threw herself onto the grass and began to sob. She was so upset that her whole body shook. I knelt down next to her and begged her to stop crying. I told her I was sorry to see her distress. She just looked up at me and explained, 'You don't understand, Pete; you just don't understand.' I tried to reassure her and finally said, 'Let me listen again. Let me try to hear. Give me another chance.'"

His eyes looked far away as he continued. "Well, while I watched, this sweet little thing pulled a rose petal out of her pocket, wiped her eyes with it, and then blew her nose to stop the sniffles. Then very bravely, she said, 'You see, Pete, I'm a genie. I've spent lifetimes in a clear bottle with no privacy at all. The very next time I got a chance to change my environment, I chose a stoneware bottle, a beautiful clay-colored one with pastel desert plants and flowers decorating it. Well, that one was even worse than the clear one. Sure I had privacy, but I was completely isolated; I couldn't see out of it to the world, and no one could see me. Hardly anyone makes wishes any more—they're too practical—and when they do, they don't run around rubbing clay bottles, so it was like being in prison. I was completely alienated.' She started to cry again, and when I put an arm around her this time, she said, 'So you see, Pete, this is my last chance. It's my third wish. If I don't pick just the right bottle, I'm finished. Whatever I choose, it's for eternity.'"

Pete had tears in his bright-blue eyes when he added, "I'll tell you; I had no idea she was homeless, and it nearly broke my heart."

"Are you sure she wasn't putting you on?" I asked him, my eyes narrowing.

"Why would she pretend she wanted a blue bottle?" he asked incredulously. "Why wouldn't she say she wanted something much bigger, much better?"

I shook my head and rolled my eyes. "I wasn't saying she was putting you on about the bottle," I explained. "I meant she was putting you on by trying to make you believe she was a genie. Everyone knows there are no such things as genies anymore."

Pete looked at me, sizing me up. "Does *everyone?*" he asked. For the first time I could hear an edge to his voice as he added, "Well now, that's pretty funny, because let me tell you, that blue bottle she found—it looked like it was made for her. Within one minute, she had slipped into it and was smiling at me through the glass. I could see that smile clear to Arizona, but the rest of her was just an outline. And she was right, you know. That blue bottle gave her privacy but it also gave her freedom. Sometimes only the people who want something know why they need it so bad. The rest of us don't have a clue."

I put my hands over my face and rubbed it, trying to wake myself up but it seemed I was as awake as I was going to get. "Maybe you're right Pete," I said. "Maybe I judged too quickly. Maybe because I don't believe in genies, I assume they no longer exist."

"It's a possibility," he said, smiling. "A *real* possibility."

"Are you mad at me now?" I asked him.

He looked surprised. "Why would I be mad at you just because you can't see something?" he asked. "You can only see what you can see."

He made it sound like I was handicapped!

Suddenly Pete sat up straight and within a moment was up on his feet again. "I have an idea," he said. "Come on."

I walked quickly behind him trying to keep up, but he was walking so fast he was almost flying. I wasn't paying much attention to where we were going until out of the corner of my eye I suddenly saw what looked like a silver gazebo. "What's that?" I said, pointing.

Pete stopped and turned immediately. "That?" he asked, pointing at the gazebo.

I nodded.

"The Fashion Pavilion," he said. "Do you want to take a look?"

"Do we have time?" I asked.

"Hey," Pete said, "We're right here. So we'll look."

I didn't see anything much until I got really close. Then I saw it: a full-length, shimmering white coat. It was so beautiful it took my breath away. I could hear my own heart beating in my ears. I could hardly contain my excitement. But then, hanging from the sleeve, I saw what I knew was the price tag. I looked at Pete, and then I reached out to read it. But suddenly afraid, I changed my mind, dropped the tag and backed away. "It's probably too expensive," I said to him.

"What do you mean?" Pete asked.

"I mean it probably costs too much," I said. "I won't be able to afford it."

Pete looked puzzled, as though he couldn't comprehend what I was saying. Then he smiled and said weakly, "We have a Careerfest going on and a Jobfest too. If you really like that Coat, I could take you to those sections."

I'm afraid I sounded impatient when I answered, "I have a job, and I have a career. I don't need either of those."

Pete looked at me, and his look was one of resignation. He held up one hand and with his other hand began to count on his fingers as he said, "You have a toaster, you have a family, you have relationships, you have a job and a career, and the only thing you want is something that you feel is bound to cost too much." He shrugged his shoulders and said impatiently, "I'm just about out of suggestions."

"Where were we going before I stopped you?" I asked, trying to get him back on track.

His eyes lit up. "You still interested in looking around?"

"I don't know," I said, "because I have no idea where you were taking me."

"Right, right," he said, but now he seemed preoccupied. Then he began to walk quickly again, and I found myself running after him.

Finally we wound up at the entrance of a beautiful green preserve. Pete raised his arm and, with a sweeping gesture, said, "This is a very special forest. It's the best we have of nature parks. There are rare birds and exotic animals, and you'll have all the peace you need. There's even a mountaintop for vision questing. You can stay until you can see, until you have a vision." Pete sounded excited, but again, I just shook my head.

"I've had visions," I protested. "I've been to other realms, and I've even had moments of enlightenment. They were eye-openers, but they're not what they're cracked up to be."

Pete just shrugged, discouraged, and we walked the rest of the way back to the entrance of the yard sale in silence. When we got back to where we'd begun, he turned to me and said, "Well, that's it."

"That's all there is?" I asked.

"No, no, no," he said. "There's much more. But you can't just go running around in all directions when you don't know what you want. Nobody has that much time."

"But I thought the secret of life was surrender," I said. "I thought it was important not to have any goals and to just let life unfold. Then the universe would provide the experiences I needed."

Pete scratched his head, messing up his already wild gray hair, and then he stared at me hard. "*That's what you thought?*" he said incredulously. "Really?"

"Yes," I said, a little miffed. "Really."

"Well, what did you think *your* part in your life was?" he asked.

"Just accepting whatever happened," I said. "With grace and dignity."

Pete frowned. "Doesn't sound like trusting the universe to me," he said. "Sounds like passing the buck."

"I can't believe you're saying this," I said. "I've spent my whole life trying to accept what life has dealt me. Not complaining. Learning. Accepting."

"Those are good things," he said. Then he looked around and seemed to be searching for something.

"What did you bring to the Yardsale?" he asked, "Hope you don't mind my asking."

"It's a yardsale," I said. "How did I know I was supposed to bring something?"

"Hey," Pete said. "You seem to know a lot. I just figured you'd know." He looked distracted when he added, "You got anything you're done with? Anything you don't want anymore? Anything somebody else can use?"

Now it was my turn to shrug my shoulders. "I don't know. Probably. I give a lot of stuff away."

"OK," Pete said. "So go home and think about what you want. Then bring back something you don't need anymore, and we'll take a walk around again."

I was a little disappointed. I wanted to come home with something. "Can't I just pick up a few things that I can afford?"

"I wouldn't suggest that," he said. "It just wastes energy. If it's not what you want, and it's not what you need, you'll just be carrying it from one place to another trying to get rid of it yourself. Unless you're into distribution, it's just extra baggage. You might as well leave it here."

"OK," I said. "Makes sense. I'll go home and really think about what I want. Then I'll come back."

Pete reached out to shake my hand, and for the first time I noticed that under his shirt sleeve, on his forearm, he had a large tattoo that said, "Jesus loves me," right in the middle of a large wreath of beautiful red roses. I pointed to it. "You're real religious, right?" I asked.

He looked down at his arm and saw what I was looking at. "Oh, not necessarily," he said. "I had that put there because I think roses are beautiful, and that's the only one they had."

"Pete," I said then, "that Coat I saw…what kind of Coat was it? Is it a Dreamcoat– like Joseph's Technicolor Dreamcoat?"

Pete shook his head. "Don't know; didn't look that closely. Besides, I get them mixed up. Can't keep track of them. You'll have to ask Rashana. She'll know. She can identify all eight of them."

"Eight? There are eight coats?" I asked.

Pete scratched his head again. He seemed to always do that when he was struggling with something he didn't know whether or not to tell me. "Eight Coats of Meaning," he muttered. "I think that's what they told me. I'm pretty sure there are eight."

"Coats of Meaning?" I said. "What does that mean?"

"Don't know. Guess it depends on which Coat you mean," he said.

He seemed to be talking in circles, and I was getting frustrated. "When are you open again?" I asked as I started to walk away.

"All of the time," Pete said. "Twenty-four hours a day, seven—it is seven, right?" I nodded, and he continued. "Seven days a week."

"How come you're open all the time?" I asked.

Pete smiled and said, "Too much trouble setting up rain dates. Can't ever tell when it's going to rain."

Rashana met me at the front gate, and she was shaking her head. She looked disappointed.

"What's wrong?" I asked her.

"I can't believe you," she said speaking quickly. "You didn't get anything? You couldn't find one thing you wanted at this enormous Yardsale? Sometimes I think I made you up; I swear." Then she quickly covered her lips as though she had cursed or something.

"Forget it," I said. "Don't worry about what you said; I won't hold it against you."

She glanced at me sideways with her eyebrows raised. "It wasn't *you* I was worrying about. You're not the only one I'm accountable to, you know."

"Oh," I said, surprised. "You mean God, right?"

"Not only God," Rashana said. "I do have teachers, you know, and supervisors, and you wouldn't believe the peer review."

"You do?" I said. "That's a very funny concept to me."

"Why?" she asked.

"Because I thought spirits and angels were perfect," I said.

Rashana shook her head. "If I were perfect, I wouldn't be doing time, and you wouldn't be on earth," she said.

"That's a very scary thought," I told her, "to be guided by someone who isn't perfect."

"Starfluff!" she said indignantly. "It's not exactly heaven to be guiding someone who isn't perfect. So we both have our crown of daisies."

I laughed. "You are truly weird," I said. "It's crown of thorns, not daisies!"

Rashana looked horrified, her silk wings fluttering. "I'm a spirit of Joy and Creativity," she told me again. "I don't do thorns."

"But I'm a soul on earth," I told her, with a false drawl, "and most people on earth—including me—do thorns."

Rashana bowed her head and put her hands together in prayer. "Lord," she said in a fervent, pleading voice, "please give me the patience, the courage, and the serenity to change this soul."

"That's not how it goes," I told her.

She looked at me. Stared would be a better word. "I was praying," she said in a voice that told me I was testing her patience. "It goes any way I want it to go."

"Well, it's not how it goes on earth," I insisted. "It goes like, 'God give me the courage to change the things I can, the patience to accept the things I cannot change, and the wisdom to know the difference.'"

"Exactly," Rashana said, and she looked very satisfied with herself.

Chapter 2
Setting the Goal

I spent the next few days obsessing about what I really wanted. What could I do that would make me happier? What did I want for myself—in concrete, physical terms? Was there anything specific I wanted that I didn't have and that would help me feel fulfilled? Was there anywhere I wanted to go or anything I wanted to do?

When I thought about the Yardsale again, all I could focus on was the magnificent Coat I had seen. Whenever I thought about it, I felt a special longing. So finally one afternoon, I meditated and called again for Rashana. She appeared dancing and skating across my mind. I stopped her long enough to tell her I'd like to see the Coat again.

"What Coat?" she asked.

"The one in the gazebo at the Yardsale," I told her.

"I must have been wandering around when Pete showed it to you."

"But if you're my higher self, my connection to spirit, you should know which one," I told her.

She lowered her head. "Did you tell me you wanted it and I forgot?"

"Well, I don't remember specifically telling you," I said. "Because I assumed you'd always know what I was doing and what I wanted."

"I come when you call," she said softly. "Your guardian angel keeps you from danger. But you're not the only life I have to live. There are others I have to watch over and guide."

"You're *my* high spirit, and you're taking care of others too?" I said, shocked.

Rashana put her hand on my shoulder. "I'm always there when you need me, but in a world of parallel universes, you're not my only soul."

"I don't understand," I said. "You're not making sense to me."

"Just take a moment and repeat what you want," she soothed. "Then we'll go together to get it."

"I don't know if it's what I want," I said. "Pete said there are Eight Coats of Meaning and that you knew about them but he didn't. He said you'd explain."

"Did you say it was hanging in a gazebo?" she asked, and I knew she didn't have a clue what I was talking about.

"Pete called it 'The Fashion Pavilion," I said. "But I thought he was putting on airs. To me it looked like a gazebo."

Suddenly Rashana laughed, and her whole expression sparkled with understanding. "Oh," she said, "Why didn't you tell me you went to the Fashion Pavilion? That clears everything up."

"Actually," I said, "I think it's pretty superficial to be talking about fashion when I'm trying to find the meaning and purpose in my life. I think I'd be a lot more comfortable if you took me a little more seriously."

Rashana looked surprised again. She grabbed her head and then said in frustration, "How can you be so dense? The Fashion Pavilion is one of the most *important* areas of the Yardsale—especially when you're talking about meaning and purpose. What do you think that Pavilion was built for?"

"How do I know?" I asked. "Pete said 'fashion.' You know, to me that means dress styles, designer clothes. Rich people."

"Oh, Father/Mother," Rashana prayed, looking up to the heavens. "How am I to work and play with someone so...human!"

Someone must have spoken in whispers in her ear because in a flash her expression changed. Suddenly she looked contrite, and her voice was soft and kind when she explained to me, "The Fashion Pavilion is the place you make the choice about the fashion in which you will live your life. It's one of the most important choices you will ever make."

I started to laugh. "Oh," I said, "*That* kind of fashion."

She smiled. "Now which Coat did you see?" she asked.

I described the Coat. "But I want to see if its what I really want. Pete said you could show me all the Coats. He said there were Eight Coats of Meaning, but he didn't remember which one that was."

"Fair enough," Rashana said, smiling. "But there's something else we have to do first, somewhere else I want to take you before we return to the Yardsale."

"OK," I said. "Still, this isn't going to be just another one of your flights of fancy, is it? I mean, even now I feel guilty because I should be writing."

"I keep being amazed at how much you've forgotten about the plans we made before this life at hand," she said. "It constantly surprises me that you have lost so much of your long-term memory."

I put my hand on my hip and stared right at her. "Look, Rashana, I really don't need to be insulted by my own higher self. There's tons of other things to bring me down, including my own insecurities. You're supposed to be cheering me up, not being a downer."

Rashana looked like she didn't know what I was talking about again. "The truth is," she said, "I was just making an observation. I checked with you, as a soul, before you ever came to earth. Then, you seemed as excited as I was. Then, you thought it was a great plan."

"Well, you might be right," I said. "But now I don't remember, and I can't be held responsible for what I don't remember agreeing to."

Rashana spun around in front of me and smiled. "Is that true?" she asked me.

"What?" I asked.

"That one isn't responsible for what one doesn't remember?"

"Well, isn't it?" I asked.

"Not where I come from," Rashana explained. "There, a deal is a deal."

"Now the fact is that I just have to take your word for it, right?" I said, getting irritated.

"Well, some part of you, aside from me, will remember in time," she said. "You have temporary amnesia, but as we go along and I explain what we're doing, it will probably jog your soul memory. That's how it works."

"What you're saying is that, in the meantime, I just have to trust you," I said.

Rashana patted my arm with reassurance. "It would probably be easier that way."

I took a deep breath. "OK," I said, resigned. "What's the next step?"

"The Computer of Manifestation at the University of Higher Thought," she said. "We have to make a plan before we can carry it through. We have to commit to it before we can help create it."

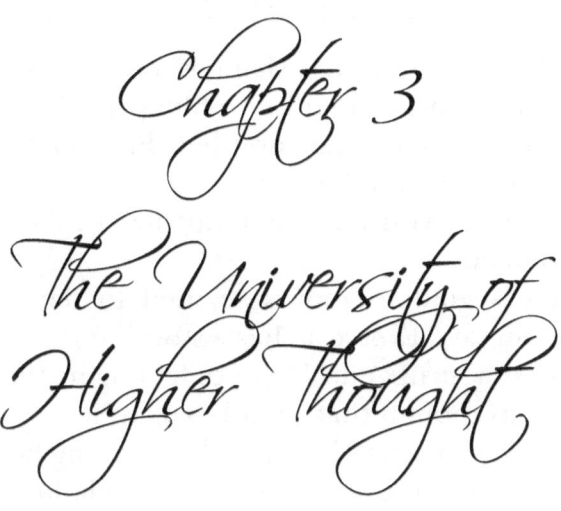

Chapter 3

The University of Higher Thought

Rashana and I stood waiting for the unicorn she called Magic. We were standing on a rainbow cloud as though waiting at a bus station.

Suddenly, Magic danced to a full stop in front of us.

I reached up to touch him, to run my fingers over his nose. He had a silver-white coat and sparkly amethyst eyes.

Rashana said, "Look at his side."

I looked and saw a golden scar across his satiny coat. "What's that from?" I asked Rashana.

"He's training with Chiron, who trained the Olympian heroes' sons, including the great healer, Aesculapius. Now, Magic is his prodigy."

I frowned. "Wasn't Chiron the wounded healer? Wasn't he the centaur that Zeus hit with his thunderbolt?"

Rashana whispered, "Magic is a direct descendant of Chiron. So it's etched in his blueprint."

Magic snorted and nodded his head. "Come, come," he said. "Jump on."

"But won't you tell me about it?" I asked him. "I want to hear."

Magic's golden hooves seemed to dance, and I heard him say, "Everyone has a story."

Rashana shrugged. "He's not feeling mythic today," she said, as though that would explain it.

We jumped on his back, Rashana riding behind me with her arms around my waist. We rode fast, upward and upward along a moving path of luminescent energy. Silver sparkles, like pebbles bouncing off a gravel driveway, were blowing all around, and one got in my eye. Suddenly I could see as though through a prism, all light sticks and shards crossing each other and casting rainbows in front of me.

I tried to wipe it away, but Rashana said, "Just wait a moment or two. It will dissolve. Silver stardust only lasts a little while, but it does change one's vision, doesn't it?" I agreed.

Magic swung to the right, to the cherubs' nest. I shook my head, and Rashana said, "No, no, Magic, not here. We need to go to the University."

Magic made a fast turn, and I almost slid off his back, but Rashana caught and steadied me.

"Front gate?" he asked. Then he added, "Want to pass the Fragment Room?"

"Don't be horsey," Rashana said to him. By her tone I knew it was an insult.

Rashana had taken me—only once—to see the Fragment Room. I never wanted to return. It was a dark and dismal warehouse, the waiting place of all aborted dreams and unfinished creations. Small, glowing, fractured thoughts and abandoned dreams flew in pieces, like tiny arms and legs, spinning in circles, banging off walls, frantically searching—like small, hungry orphans—for someone to claim them so they could become part of something larger and feel complete. It was one of the few places in the upper realms that made me feel scared and sad.

Finally we arrived at the University of Higher Thought.

When Rashana and I slid off Magic's back in front of the Creative Communication Center, we found the gate padlocked with a shiny golden lock.

"Now what?" I asked.

Rashana was shaking her head. "I'll use the telecom and see if Eva can let us in."

"Who's that?" I asked.

She put her finger to her lips and whispered, "You'll be so excited to meet her. She has real nobility of spirit." Then she walked over to a small round disk painted like the sun on the left side of the gate and pushed its center. I swear I heard a harp. Then Rashana asked, "Can we come in for just a moment?"

The lock fell away, and Rashana and I scaled the steps to the front door. Eva was waiting there, and she smiled as she let us in. She was beautiful and looked more like a goddess than an angel—more like Venus than Gabriel. She was dark and slender and wore a long, flowing gown of light silk held closed by gold satin roping.

"Is she an angel?" I whispered to Rashana as we entered.

"She's a high healer and counselor, a member of the Core Group of Healers closest to the One," Rashana explained. "She's also the High Spirit in Charge of the Gifted but Difficult Spirit/Souls."

I wrinkled my nose. "She's a special ed Spirit?" I asked. "Why is she here?" Rashana tilted her head and whispered, "She's a healing counselor, and she's our supervisor."

"Oh," I said, and then I swear I heard organ music as Rashana introduced us.

"Creating something?" Eva asked us and smiled. A light aura of purple emanated from her body.

Rashana looked at me, waiting for me to answer, and when I didn't, she turned to Eva and said, "I imagine so."

"Is she a good teacher?" I whispered to Rashana.

Rashana said, "She wouldn't be here if she wasn't good. But she's not as gentle in her counsel as some. Still, she specializes in relationships like ours. She's a healer of the highest kind so she builds in the best outcome."

I felt like I was in Catholic school all over again, being taught by nuns. Still, I liked Eva. There was something safe and comforting about her.

In the lab, Rashana and I stood in front of the Computer of the Grand Design. It was so large I couldn't even reach the keys, so Rashana brought a step stool over for me to stand on. But I couldn't decide what to type in, what to ask for, what to write about, or what I wanted. So Rashana moved me over to the smaller Computer of Manifestation, and we sat on a bench next to each other.

I'm the one who had to do the typing. Rashana tried to encourage me to type in my wishes. Anything. Something. After I sat for several more minutes with fingers frozen on the keyboard, Rashana looked at me probingly.

"What?" I asked.

"Make a wish," she said. "Just type it into the computer."

I put my hands on the keyboard. But my fingers hesitated. My mind went blank. "I can't wish," I said. "I mean, I don't know what I wish."

Rashana looked at me with disbelief and said, "Even the most talented fairy godmother can't make a wish come true if you don't wish it!" Then she looked frustrated, got down off the bench, and began to pace. "Here I am on a Creative Ray given the opportunity to help make wishes come true, and who do I have with me? A soul who can't make a wish! I don't get it! It must be some kind of a cosmic joke."

"Wait a minute," I said. "Don't give up on me. Have some patience. I'll think of something." I searched for something to want, something important enough to use a wish on. Finally, I thought I had it. "Peace in the world!" I said. "I'll wish for peace on earth."

Rashana made a face at me. She wasn't pleased. "Can't you ever mind your own business?" she asked. "I'm offering you a wish, a wish for you, not for everyone else in the world. They have their own plans, and we can't interfere."

I thought about it. "I can't do it," I said. "I'd like to, but with all the suffering in the world, I can't think of anything I want just for me."

"Great," she said. "If all the other souls in the world felt like you do, we'd have an eternal stalemate. No one wishes. No one creates. Nothing gets done."

"Maybe it's writer's block," I suggested.

Then, with a look of impatience, Rashana turned away.

Suddenly Eva was standing alongside us. She addressed Rashana, asking patiently, "Would you like to check with the Angel Council of the All-As-One?"

Rashana smiled and looked relieved. "I can't do anything with her this way," she said, throwing up her hands in a gesture of futility.

We left the University and followed Eva over to the Administration Building. We walked the long corridor until we reached the brilliant offices of the Heavenly Hosts and Hostesses. Before we even knocked, the door to the Angel Council opened with the soft sound of celestial music.

We walked in.

It was the first time Rashana had ever taken me to the University Special Sessions of the Angel Council, and I felt awestruck and mildly uncomfortable. Several majestic Archangels were seated at a large luminescent wafer, like a theater in the Round. A chorus of smaller angels stood behind them.

Rashana and I walked up and stood Center Circle–like Center Stage–until the pink spotlight shone on us. Then Rashana spoke. "This soul can't remember how to make a wish. She can't decide what she wants. When I formulated the original plans, I never imagined a human living without wishes, so I'm embarrassed to admit I didn't formulate a solution for this problem. I can't go any further. Can you help?"

One of the young training angels was placing coasters on the surface of the light table while another training angel walked behind pouring out holy water for the Archangels to drink. Then each Archangel was given a pile of powder.

"What's that?" I whispered to Rashana.

"Angel dust," she whispered back.

"Drugs?" I said. "Angels do *drugs*?"

"Not *that* kind of angel dust," she said. "The mills of the gods grind slowly, but they grind exceedingly fine. This is the dust of the goodness of humans who lived their lives fully and made the transition to spirit gracefully. Their dust is added to the All-Knowledge to enrich it and provide a universal source for the regeneration of future human beginnings. But first it must be blessed by the Angel Counselors."

"You mean this is what that expression means?" I said. "The old 'dust to dust' saying?" Now it sounded like a compost pile.

Rashana smiled and shook her head. "I thought you knew."

As we waited, center stage, both of us fidgeting, one of the largest archangels stood up from the surround, walked up to where we stood, and whispered in Rashana's ear.

Suddenly Rashana beamed. "Thank you," she said. "Truly, we thank you."

Then Rashana grabbed my hand and flew me out of the Council room, through the hallway, down the steps of the university, and out the gate to where Magic was waiting, tapping his golden hoof.

"Take us back to the Yardsale, please," Rashana said.

Magic snorted with the sound of flute music when we jumped upon his back again.

"Why are you suddenly so excited about going back to the Yardsale?" I asked. "What section are you taking me to now?"

"You'll see," Rashana said, as Magic took flight.

Chapter 4

Choices

Pete, dressed in a doorman's outfit, was waiting outside the white picket fence of the Yardsale when we arrived. His curly gray hair was pulled back neatly under his cap, but he was still wearing his necklace with its colorful beads falling in long strands over his chest and his silver peace pendant. He greeted us gallantly and bowed as he held the gate open for us.

"Where are you taking me?" I asked Rashana again.

Rashana looked pleased with herself. "Over to the Adoption Center," she said. She looked at me and gently placed her hand on my shoulder. "We're going to redo your childhood. This time, you pick the parents, the lifetime, the childhood that you want. It's a gift."

"What's this all about?" I asked her. "Is this what they mean by being 'born again'?" I felt myself smiling. I had no idea what Rashana was doing.

"After this, you'll know what you want," she reassured me. Then she tickled me. "Wait till you see all the choices you have."

It was a beautiful day at the Yardsale, with blue birds singing and the golden sun shining bright on the vibrant green grass. Rashana held my hand as we raced down to a small body of water, a cool bubbling brook with silver fish jumping up into the air and chasing each other from one end to the other.

"Pick a country," Rashana said. "Just close your eyes and pick some place you'd like to be."

"Ireland. A house in Ireland," I said, and I was immediately transported there. I walked around over bright green, rolling hills until I saw a small, cozy cottage. Then, like Goldilocks, I slowly opened the creaky door and went inside.

In the kitchen at a large, rough-hewn wooden table in front of a warm, crackling fireplace, there sat a middle-aged man and woman. They were laughing and talking to each other happily.

"I wish we had a child," the woman said. "Just one. That would make me completely happy."

The man smiled. "This life is not meant for too much happiness," he said. "Be content. We have each other." He reached out to hold her hand. She smiled. But under his breath, I heard him say, "Of all the things I wish, I wish this hardest of all. Still, maybe it's just too much to ask."

Rashana smiled. "They seem very nice," she said. "You'd have a happy life here. A child is the only wish they have. You could make their one wish come true."

A part of me traveled forward and could see my life with these fine people. Catered to, close to nature, attended to and fussed over all the time. But I looked around the house for books and saw none. I thought of feeding cows and chopping wood and decided. "No," I said. "Not here."

"Venice?" Rashana suggested. "What about Venice? There's a loving couple there, a professor of music and his wife. They are kind and loving, though a little strict and rigid. They have books. You would learn to play piano. You could sing."

Again, within a blink, I was there, in Venice. I found myself in the living room of a pastel pink stucco house seated on pilings surrounded by water. The couple living here was a little different, richer, slightly sterner, with not as much love between them as the Irish couple but still both with a fervent wish for a child. They'd prayed for it over and over again. I looked at Rashana. "No," I said, "Not here either."

To France then, to Cannes, to the most beautiful seaside I'd ever seen. Now I was looking at the clear blue Mediterranean, the azure sky, and the sailboats. There were beaches crowded with happy young people running around, laughing, and having fun. On one of the blankets, I saw a young couple. I heard them whisper in French to each other, loving secrets, hidden longings, and somehow I understood. They too wanted a child. They wanted to share their perfect love. I took a deep breath. I loved the sound and the feel of the place. I really liked the couple. But I told Rashana, "No, not here either."

"Is there something wrong with all these couples?" she asked.

"Nothing at all," I said. "They all seem like lovely people. I'm sure I'd have a lovely life. The countries are beautiful, the houses are comfortable, and I don't doubt they would be good to any child they had. But it can't be me. I'd never have learned all I did unless I grew up with my own parents and lived my own life."

"You mean you have no complaints?" she asked. "You wouldn't rather live somewhere else, trade your difficult childhood for an easier one, be loved more unconditionally, and have greater freedom?"

"I didn't say that," I told her. "But I learned from the way I was brought up, the 'conditional' way my parents loved me, and the obstacles I've encountered in my life. I even learned from the things my parents did wrong with me. Because I loved them in spite of the injuries they caused me, I could forgive myself later when I made a lot of my own mistakes. They taught me that too. I had to search for the reasons for my difficulties within myself. I had to take responsibility for them, but once I understood, I realized that it was my parents and my whole family, with all their human frailty, that taught me and helped me grow into who I am. And so, if you don't mind, I'd rather keep my own family and my own life, flawed as it might seem to you."

"To *me?*" Rashana said, horrified. "I'm the spirit who helped you set up the situation to begin yourself with. Why would *I* think it was flawed?"

"Well, I just assumed if you wanted to take me to the Adoption Center, you wanted me to be different than I am."

Rashana stopped short. She looked at me. "I wanted you to be able to make a wish," she said, "so I could make it come true. That's what I wanted."

"Well, you might have to practice being a fairy godmother with someone else," I said, irritated. "Because actually, my life is my wish come true. It's turned out better than I had ever hoped it would."

Rashana shook her head and rolled her eyes. "I know a zillion other spirits who would congratulate themselves for having a soul who would say that. But I want you to see the healing in beauty. I want you to be able to wish, and I want you to stop the suffering you keep doing."

"Why?" I asked. "I enjoy my suffering. It makes me feel like a sensitive human being."

With Rashana tried again to explain. "I am a Spirit of Joy and Creativity. You are my soul on earth at this time. How are we going to go forward toward wholeness if you insist on clinging to your suffering?"

"I understand your problem," I said. "But I'm sure if you give me some more time, I'll be ready to change my mind, and I'll be able to wish for a million things I don't have. Life will get too hard again, and I'll want you around. In the meantime, honestly, I'm having a good time."

Rashana and I were walking out of the Yardsale when she asked, "What do you want to be when you grow up?"

"*Me*," I said. Then I stopped and asked her, "Do spirits grow up? And if they do, what do *you* want to be?"

Rashana looked thoughtful, and then she said, "Spirits are always growing and changing, but I guess when I grow up and change enough, I'd still like to be me."

We both stopped dead in our steps, stunned. At that same moment, we both understood.

"Oh, Jezzwhistle!" Rashana said. "We've been seeing 'me' to 'me' instead of 'I' to 'I' all this time."

"What does it mean?" I asked. "Are we in trouble?"

She put her arm around my shoulders and pulled me closer. "We're not warriors any longer," she said. "We're dancers now, but we've been dancing back to back, with our arms folded in front of us. Each of us has been looking at different things, having different visions, seeing different worlds. Unless we turn to face each other, unless we change some steps, neither of us will even understand what the other sees. You'll be looking through soul eyes on earth, and I'll being looking through spirit eyes in the heavens, and we'll never do what we came to earth to do."

"Which is?" I asked.

"Creative writing," she said.

"You're going to make me crazy," I told her. "I want to do healing. I've told you that a hundred times at least. I want you to see the beauty in healing, the beauty in human nature even if there is suffering. It's earthly beauty that I see."

Now Rashana faced me, and she was running her fingers through her long, blond hair, making a mess of it. "I want to show you the healing in beauty," she said. "Because that's heavenly. I accept that you love healing. But can't you see the part you're missing?"

"Of course not," I said. "How could I? If I'm missing it, I can't see it."

"That's my part," she said, softening her gaze. "Helping you see."

"What?" I asked.

"Let me ask you something," she said. "Who do you want to heal?"

"Everyone," I said. "Everyone who's suffering."

Rashana's eyes softened even more, and her whole look was one of compassion. "What about you?" she asked.

"What about me?" I asked.

"Physician, heal thyself," she said.

"I'm a nurse," I said.

"Stop nitpicking," Rashana said.

But she had made her point. I had never considered that "healing" might have meant healing myself. And that in order to heal anyone, I had to become whole, and that meant integrating all aspects of myself.

"I get it," I told Rashana.

"You'd never know it by looking at you," she said.

I looked at her. "Spirits are not supposed to be wise guys," I said.

Rashana looked at me, her brow wrinkled. "Spirits aren't *supposed* to be anything," she said. "But when they are—they're really something! Plus the best thing a spirit can be is a wise guide." Now, Rashana wore an expression of renewed commitment. "I'll work it out," she reassured me. "Don't worry. Trust me. I'll figure it out for us."

I frowned. "I thought *we* would figure it out was the plan," I reminded her. "I'll teach you to see the beauty in healing, and you'll teach me to see the healing in beauty."

"Now, there's a symphony!" she said, excited. "The song you are singing is the song of a healer and the dance you are doing is one of joy! But I have only one more question to ask you right now."

"OK, do it," I said. "Especially if it will help me make a wish."

"When we started all of this, you began by saying you wanted to save the world, or at least help heal your planet, right?" she asked. But before I could answer, she added with great urgency, "Can you see that you're beginning to live in an unstoried world? Can you see that most of the stories are recycled from a different time? Earth and the beings on it have outgrown them. Unless there are new stories created to map the journey into new worlds, unless there are new hopes and values, the species and the planet will die, or at the very least it will stunt growth for too long a time."

"How do you make that sound like a vitamin deficiency?" I asked. "Or worse?"

Rashana put her hands on my shoulders and turned me toward her. She looked me straight in the eye when she said, "The future of earth depends on human beings' ability to imagine it," she said. "They have forgotten how to use their imaginations to create, and they are losing hope."

"Well, aren't the spirit realms trying to help us?" I asked. "Or why aren't other planets that are more evolved trying to help us?"

"Soulee," she said fondly, "each must play the part they promised. We must create our stories to honor our promise, because a promise is a path. Creative writing and healing was our vow. If we do it right, our stories can heal!"

I took a deep breath. "OK," I said. "I'll try to come up with something to write. But maybe the next time we meet, we could go over to the Fashion Pavilion, and I could look for that coat I saw? I know it has something to do with our purpose. I just know if I try it on, I'll get it!"

Chapter 5

The Coat of Armor

The next two weeks passed quickly, and life around my house seemed to settle down. My schedule had gotten more manageable, and I even had some time to relax. So I was lying on the couch in my living room listening to some soft New Age music and feeling very relaxed when it suddenly hit me.

"OK," I said aloud, finally giving in. "It's true. I can't live another day without seeing that Coat again. I have to know more about it, what it was that fascinated me about it, and what it really costs. Somehow it got under my skin."

Within moments Rashana was dancing in front of me, lightly, lithely, and gracefully. "I'll take you back to the Yardsale if you want to go," she said happily.

"But I don't want to walk around and look at anything else," I told her. "I want to go straight to the gazebo and really look at that coat again."

Then I remembered what Pete had said about bringing something to the Yardsale that I was finished with. I finally dug into the bottom of one of my closets and pulled out an old pair of boots. Old combat boots. "But what will anyone want with these?" I asked aloud, holding them up into the air.

Rashana said, "Your purpose is joy and creativity now, but there are those who are still living as Spirit Warriors in areas of consciousness with rough terrain, and they're doing difficult work that requires those boots. Someone will be grateful to have them."

And so, reassured, I carried my boots and went with Rashana to the Yardsale.

Pete was standing there as always, leaning against the fence, carefully shining an old piece of silverware until the rays of the sun bounced off it in radiant rainbow reflections lighting his face and making him smile.

"Howdy," he said. "See you brought some good boots." He reached out to take them from me. "Were they comfortable? Did you like them?"

"I did," I said. "I loved them. I wore them for years; they were my favorites. They kept my feet warm through a lot of cold and stormy nights."

"Great," he said. "Then they're a real gift, because love softens and strengthens the leather. They'll make someone else's steps lighter as they trudge through the mud on their stormy nights. Now these boots know the way through the darkness to the Light and they'll take that knowing with them to offer to whomever wears them next."

Pete smiled at me as he took the cloth he had been using to shine the silver and began to shine my boots. Right in front of my eyes, as I watched in amazement, those boots began to look like the magical blue leather boots of a Spiritual Warrior. "Thanks," he added, as Rashana and I walked past him into the Yardsale.

Rashana seemed to know exactly where she was going as she walked with determination toward the Fashion Pavilion. I huffed and puffed as I tried to keep up with her.

When we were standing in front of the gazebo, both of us stared at the one empty hanger that was left. I was crushed. "Oh my God," I said. "Somebody took my Coat!"

Rashana frowned and looked at me. "That's not possible," she reassured. "If it was yours, it would still be here. There are no accidents. Nothing that really belongs to you can be taken by another."

"Well, where is it then?" I asked.

Rashana stared hard at the hanger. Suddenly there appeared a long, light not quite white Coat.

I looked at it and I frowned. "That's not the coat I saw," I said. My heart sank with disappointment. This Coat was rough and heavy looking.

"How do you know?" she said.

I walked up the gazebo steps and reached out to touch the coat. It was not quite white, that was true, but it felt like linen or muslin. It was stiff and hard with a thick and heavy insulation for a lining. "It doesn't feel right," I told Rashana. "It's the wrong coat."

"You're sure?" she asked. "It will protect you from the elements, and its got great lining. No wind or rain or hail or flying pebbles will penetrate it."

"I don't like it," I told her. "In fact, I *really* don't like it."

Rashana frowned. "Why don't you at least try it on and see how it feels?" she asked. "You really can't tell how something will look when it's on the hanger."

I thought about it. "OK," I said. "I'll try it on."

Rashana pulled it off the hanger and helped me put it on and button it up.

"Jeez," I said, my shoulders sagging under the weight of it. "This Coat feels even more awful than I imagined. I can hardly move in it. It weighs a ton. The elements may not get to me, but neither will the touch of another human or the warmth of the sun." Then I looked at her again. "You'd hate me wearing it. I certainly couldn't dance in it; it's much too restrictive." I tried to stretch my arms out, but the lining, like a straightjacket, stopped me dead.

Rashana looked at me with a twinkle in her eyes and a slightly amused expression on her lips but said nothing, so I began to try to take off the Coat. But the buttons wouldn't come undone. I almost had to rip them off. "Please help me take this off?" I asked Rashana. "Hurry! I'm beginning to feel smothered. I can't breathe."

Rashana, with almost no effort, had the coat off me in a minute. Then she said, "So you're certain?"

"Certain?" I said. "I'm more than certain. I can't imagine why anyone would make a Coat like that. Or why anyone would wear a Coat like that. Or why anyone would even want a Coat like that. What kind of a Coat is it, anyway? What's it made of?"

Rashana put the Coat back on the hanger, but before she would allow me to be finished with it, she said, "You really should check the price tag."

"Why?" I asked. "I don't like that Coat. I wouldn't wear it if someone paid me!"

She looked at me and simply said, "Comparison shopping."

I reached for the price tag and read it aloud. "Authenticity and Intimacy." I shivered. "I don't get it," I said.

Rashana sat down on the grass. It was a beautiful day, and the sun was warm and comforting. She patted a place next to her for me to sit.

I sat down and asked, "Do you think the other Coat, the one I love, is gone?" In that moment, I felt such longing it was almost painful.

Rashana smiled. "Don't know," she said. "You'll have to decide when I show you the others. But we have to answer one question at a time. What do you want to know first?"

My whole body shivered as though I had a chill. "What kind of a Coat is this one?" I pointed to the Coat I had just tried on. It was now lying in a heap on the Pavilion floor.

"That's the Coat of Armor, Carol," Rashana said softly. "An updated version of the Coat of Fear. It's made up of defenses used when someone is frightened and feels threatened and when they feel they need protection. It's woven with threads of anger and hurt, sewn with the rigid strings of arrogance and alienation, and trimmed with sarcasm and harsh words."

"Oh, how awful," I said.

But Rashana put her fingers to her lips. "Don't judge it as 'bad,'" she insisted. "For those who've been hurt, it does offer protection. It serves them. It gives their deep wounds time to heal. That Coat is only restrictive if once it has served its purpose, it continues to be worn. Then it can inhibit growth. Then, it becomes negative."

"But this is a Yardsale," I said, trying to digest what she had told me. "So it must have belonged to someone who donated it. It's not a child's coat, so someone must have really walked through life wearing it. I can't imagine how they could have done it even for a little while. I feel bad."

Rashana smiled at me with compassion.

"Do you know who that Coat belonged to?" I asked her.

She nodded.

"Can you tell me without breaking any spirit rules?" I asked.

"Yes," she said. "I can do it without breaking any rules, but I don't know whether I can do it without breaking your heart. Are you sure you want to know?"

"Oh yes," I said. "I do."

Rashana moved closer and put her arm around my shoulders. "It was yours, Soulee, and you wore it for a very long time."

Chapter 6

The Dream Coat

Rashana seemed distracted the next time I saw her. I had been meditating and suddenly, there she was again. This time she was dressed in a wrinkled, blue cotton angel outfit that looked as though she had just thrown it on in a hurry. Even her wings and her halo were crooked, but her expression was absolutely divine. She didn't notice me. She was cloud dancing again, looking down at her feet. She did a kind of funny little dance on just the tips of her toes as she tilted her head from side to side in reaction to some inner celestial music I was sure she was hearing. I didn't want to interrupt her, but I wanted her to know I was there.

I coughed a couple of times, and when she finally looked up and saw me, all I said was, "Hi. I was trying to meditate, and I guess I must have landed on the wrong channel."

Rashana giggled. "Right channel," she said. And then she asked, "Do you want to go to a Fashion Pavilion again?"

"You're kidding, right?" I said. "You mean to try on another Coat?"

Rashana covered her mouth with her hand so I knew she was laughing at me again. "See, you're beginning to understand. We're communicating!"

I frowned. "Is this time going to be as hard for me?" I asked. "I mean like finding out about the Coat of Armor?"

"It should be interesting," she said. "Maybe for you, even exciting. Some of the pain you felt over the Coat of Armor was because it was a Coat you had already outgrown. It's always painful to go backward."

"Can I see the Dream Coat next?" I asked. "And can you tell me the names of the other coats?"

Rashana smiled. "We'll ask the Designer."

This time when Rashana and I arrived at the Fashion Pavilion, an elegant-looking woman dressed in a simple white gown and wearing a flowing white chiffon scarf over her head was walking around the center of the bare wooden Pavilion floor in gold high heels. She was stunning.

Surrounding her, several beautiful Coats were spinning in front of me on a sparkling carousel.

"Who's that?" I whispered to Rashana, pointing.

"The Fashion Designer," Rashana answered. "Otherwise known as the Uppity Angel."

I frowned. "You're kidding, right?"

"No," she said. "Why would you believe I was kidding?"

"Come on," I said.

Then she stopped and said, "She really is an angel. The Uppity Angel, to be exact. Very creative."

"Did you say 'uppity'?" I asked and hesitated. "Those two words don't seem to go together, 'uppity' and 'angel.'"

Rashana looked at me with a puzzled expression. "Why?" she asked. "She created the Coats and with each Coat that fits, the soul grows or rises, like—goes up—on the spiral of evolution. So what better angel to create them than the Uppity Angel?"

I put my hands up in front of me in a gesture of surrender. "OK," I said. "That's it. If she wants to be called the Uppity Angel, then that's what I'll call her."

Rashana frowned. "Her name is EuphiU. So, now that I've told you her name, maybe it will help. Sometimes when you know where someone comes from, you know a little more about them."

"Except that knowing her name doesn't give me a clue about where she comes from," I explained.

Rashana looked stunned. "Now, *you're* kidding, right?"

I shook my head.

"EuphiU is a creative spirit," she said. "Her name indicates her vibration, her frequency—which, my sweet little soul, is like knowing someone's address on earth."

"I still don't get it," I said. "How does it follow that her name indicates her vibration?"

"It all adds up," she said. "It adds up to the number eight, which means she's located on Ray 8."

"I don't have a clue how you did that," I said.

Rashana held up her fingers as though teaching a child to add one and one as she spoke. "A =1, B=2, C=3 and so forth. Then you add them up to eight. Once you know that number, you know the Ray that

Spirit comes from. It's like knowing the neighborhood someone comes from."

"Not if I don't have any idea what the Rays are," I said.

Rashana put her hand to her lips in a gesture of surprise. "I thought you knew about the Ray Chart," she said.

"You want to explain it to me?" I asked.

Rashana shook her head. "Not now," she said. "Maybe later. When we do the book *The Therapeutic Uses of the Ray Chart.* Right now we have other important things to do. We have to shop."

She turned toward the Pavilion again and tiptoed up to stand beside the Uppity Angel. They said a few things to each other, and I saw EuphiU wink.

Then Rashana came back down to stand beside me. "EuphiU said she'll clear the Pavilion and display the coats she designed for you, if you like."

"All of them?" I asked. "All at once?"

Rashana said, "It was our choice how we wanted to do it."

"What was our choice?" I asked, confused. "What's the alternative?"

"I could tell you the names of all the Coats. She would show them all at once, or she would show them one at a time, and I could explain, like in a fashion show," Rashana said.

"OK," I said, "Let's do them one at a time from the least important to the most, until I've seen all of them."

"That's not a choice," Rashana said.

"What are you talking about?" I asked. "I thought that's what you just said."

Rashana shook her head. "Well, that's not what I said. I said nothing about least important or most important. I didn't place them in any kind of order. I never made one better than another. That wouldn't be my truth. They're all different. All are of equal value."

"Well then how will I choose what to see first?" I asked.

"Choice is subjective," she said. "What do you want to see first?"

"I don't know," I told her. "I don't even know what kind of Coats there are. I also don't know what each Coat costs so I have no way of selecting."

Rashana looked at me. "Certainly we still have a different vision because I don't know how it could matter where on a spiral we begin as long as we see the entire spiral."

"Oh," I said. "You said these Coats had to do with evolution. I thought we were climbing the ladder of evolution. That means there are steps. 'Ladder' is what it's usually called on earth, you know."

"Why?" she asked. "If wholeness, balance, and integration of all aspects is the—pardon the expression—goal of the soul, then how can it matter which comes first?"

"I don't know how you do that," I said, getting impatient. "You always twist things around."

"I'm just explaining how I see it," she said.

I got frustrated, so I got snappy again. "Just tell me the names, and then I'll choose."

Rashana smiled. "I'll be happy to," she said. "Do you want to sit down?" Suddenly a park bench appeared, and she sat. I sat down next to her.

"Sorry I was impatient," I said. "It's just that I get frightened when I get confused."

"I know," she said simply, but when she smiled, I felt better.

The Fashion Pavilion had been cleared while we'd been talking, and now the plain, shiny oak floor was bare. I looked for Uppity Angel but didn't see her.

"Who's going to model them?" I asked.

Rashana said, "Oh, there are a lot of models for each coat."

"Well, a lot can't model it at once," I said. "I mean who's going to wear it to show it to me?"

Rashana frowned. "These are meant for you. They are originals. No one but you can wear them."

I took a deep breath. Then I looked around the Yardsale and watched as Pete passed by with his head down. Though I knew he saw us, he didn't say a word.

"Hi, Pete," I shouted, but he never looked up.

"Uh oh," Rashana said.

"Something's wrong with Pete?" I said.

"Wrong? No, I don't think that's possible," she said. "But it sure looks like something's troubling him."

"Shouldn't we see what it is?" I asked.

"Not before we do our own work," Rashana said in a no-nonsense voice.

"OK," I said. "Then let's get down to business. Name the Coats please, so I can choose."

Rashana closed her eyes and folded her hands in front of her as though in prayer. While she spoke she stayed in that position and seemed to be listening to something or someone. "One, the Coat of Armor; two, the Dream Coat; three, the Coat of Trust; four, the Coat of Truth; five, the Coat of Change; six, the Coat of Love; seven, the Radiant Coat of Death; and eight, the Coat of All." Then she opened her eyes and smiled at me. "Nice assortment," she added.

I laughed. "OK," I said. "Let me see them in order. So next I'll look at the Dreamcoat."

"I didn't do them in any order," she reminded. "I just did them."

"Well, let's pretend the way you said them is the way they go," I said. "Is that acceptable?"

"Of course," she said.

So Rashana stood up and called, "The Dream Coat, please?"

As though it were magic, the coat appeared. It was more beautiful than I had remembered it, and the colors were shimmering, pastel, and almost alive with movement. It had sequins and threads of gold throughout and lots of silver stars that blinked.

"Feel it," Rashana suggested.

"May I?" I asked.

"How can you tell if you want something except by how you feel about it?" she asked.

I reached out and touched the Coat. It was light as a summer's breeze and smooth as still water. Then I saw the price tag.

"Look at it," Rashana said. "Or how are you going to know what you'll have to pay for it?"

"I'm nervous about it," I said. "What if it costs too much? Then I won't be able to have it, and I'll be disappointed."

"That's true," she said. "And it's that disappointment that will keep you growing until you can pay the price."

Tentatively, I lifted the tag and read it. "Price: 3-D Reality" was highlighted.

"What does that mean?" I asked.

Rashana's expression was noncommittal. "It means while you're wearing it, you can't live in an ordinary world of reality as you've been used to. It's a Dream coat after all. Don't you want to try it on?"

"I don't know," I said. "After that last Coat..."

Rashana said, "This Coat isn't heavy like the last. In fact, it's quite light."

"Okay," I said, as she lifted it off the hanger. "I'll try it."

I put my arm in one sleeve and had to struggle to get the other arm in. Though once it was on, I could hardly feel it. "Do you have a mirror?" I asked. "So I can see how it looks?"

Suddenly EuphiU appeared, and hanging in the air next to her was a full-length mirror. I looked at myself. "Good God," I said, seeing that the Coat was well above my knees and the sleeves were up around my elbows. "This is a little kid's coat. This is all wrong. It doesn't even come close to fitting. I can't wear this. It looks awful on me."

Both Rashana and the Uppity Angel were now frowning. "That's a lovely Coat," Rashana said.

I repeated, a little too self-righteously, "It's a child's coat."

EuphiU agreed. "That's true," she said. "It is. Children have the most beautiful dreams and visions. They can move from one place to another so lightly that they can see all the different worlds. It's perfect."

I looked at both of them. "Just give it to a child then," I said. "Because it doesn't fit me now." I figured that Rashana was going to pull one of those deals she had the time before with the Coat of Armor. So I tried to outsmart her. "And if you're going to tell me it was mine," I said, "I'm going to tell you I've outgrown it."

Rashana looked at EuphiU, and then she looked at me with an expression of real sadness in her eyes. "No, Carol," she said. "It was never yours. That Coat could take you to a place of delicate dreams and magical myths. It could take you to lands of fantasy with all the happily ever afters that have ever been. It's so light that it can lift almost any child right out of the kind of suffering that exists on earth. It's one of the most precious coats there is. It's one of my favorites. But I am truly sorry to say that it never really fit you."

EuphiU came over to me and rearranged the sleeves. "Wear it," she said. "Don't just put it on." Then she extended her arms and began to move side to side in graceful, flowing movement as though she was dancing. "Try this," she said.

I began to do what she had asked, and right before my eyes as I looked in the mirror, the Coat began to grow to fit me.

Rashana smiled. "Now, try this," she said. And she began her cloud-dancing step. I followed her.

Then she said, "Now move your arms like an eagle's wings." I did, and I felt the light winds of change moving me toward freedom.

"Move your legs like a cat does," she said, and when I did, I felt a strange stirring in my belly, a strange remembering.

"Now lasso a star," she said, holding her hand above her head and making circles in the air. When I did that, I laughed. It felt wonderful. When I looked in the mirror now, though the Coat was still short, the rest of it fit perfectly.

I shrugged. "I could get away with it, I guess," I said.

"That's the point," Rashana said. "Wear it on warm summer days when you run through the grass. Wear it to dance and to dream in. It offers no protection—that's not why you want to wear it—but it does offer a certain freedom and vision, and that's its most price-less quality."

I took off the Dream Coat, and Rashana and I went back to sit on the bench. "You're right," I told her. "That Coat feels better on than it looks off."

Rashana smiled. "Want to see the Coat of Trust next?" she asked.

"No," I said. "You said the Coat of Truth comes next."

Rashana shook her head. "Well, if I said that, then I got them mixed up. I think it's better if you try on the Coat of Trust first."

"I don't want to," I said. "I want to try on the Coat of Truth. You said the order didn't make a difference."

"I said one wasn't more or less important," Rashana corrected.

I huffed and puffed, and finally she called EuphiU and asked for the Coat of Truth.

"You mean the Coat of Trust, don't you?" she asked Rashana.

"Nope," Rashana said, pointing to me. "Soulee here wants Truth before Trust, and she has free will, so let's show her what she wants."

Chapter 7
The Coat of Truth

I should have known enough by Rashana's tone to listen to her, but, of course, I didn't. Instead I insisted
on having it my own way. I noticed the look on the
Uppity Angel's face, which should have indicated I was
heading in the wrong direction; still, I ignored that
too. I wanted it the way I wanted it, and that was that.
I didn't want to see the Coat of Trust first; I wanted to
see the Coat of Truth.

The Uppity Angel had taken the Dream Coat back
to the waiting room of the Pavilion to hold it until we
finished shopping.

It seemed to take a while for her to come back, and
when she did and she looked at me, I suddenly knew
why they called her the Uppity Angel.

She took a long time to clear the platform. She
seemed to be moving in slow motion. She even used a
white feather duster to sweep the bare floor of the dust
balls that seemed to be blowing around, chasing each
other. I watched as she swept them into a dustpan and
dumped them into a large container.

Rashana and I were again sitting on the bench in front of the Pavilion waiting to see the Coat of Truth. She wasn't talking much.

"Where did all those dust balls come from?" I asked her, trying to break the tension. She had relented, but not gracefully.

"They're not dust balls," she said simply, trying to hide the chill in her voice. "They're dandelion puff-balls, the ones that were blown up to the heavens with people's wishes attached."

"Does that mean those wishes will come true?" I asked.

Rashana looked at me as though I was learning impaired. "EuphiU is sweeping them off the plat-form into a big Wishbin," she said in a tired, patient voice. "Would you sweep up something and put it in a Wishbin if you wanted it saved? Does it look to you like those are the wishes that will come true?"

I got huffy. "Stop treating me as though I'm dis-abled," I said. "I have no idea what happens to the stuff in the Wishbin so I can't imagine whether they're saved or dumped. Therefore, there is no way I could know."

Rashana sighed. "Okay," she said, "The missing clue. The 'stuff,' as you call it—in the Wishbin—gets recycled like everything else. Does that help?"

"Not a bit," I said.

Rashana softened. "Wishes that are meant to come true are placed at the end of the rainbow, not in a Wishbin," she said.

I was horrified. "You mean even if our wishes reach heaven, they're sometimes dumped in a trashcan?"

"Of course," Rashana said. "Have you ever heard some of the wishes that people make? People wish for revenge. They make wishes for power. They wish for things that can completely divert them from their purpose. Not good for the soul or All. What would you have us do with them?"

"Save them?" I asked.

"Everything doesn't have to be saved. Some things need to be discarded, or else a soul cannot grow. If bad wishes aren't trashed, how can good wishes come true?"

I was getting tired of all the philosophy. "Where's the Coat of Truth?" I asked.

"I've given you some time to consider if it's still the one you want to see," she said. "But if you're certain—"

I cut her off. "I'm certain. I'm sure. I've made up my mind. I want to see it," I said.

Rashana called to EuphiU. Within minutes the Coat appeared.

I ran up to the platform to make sure I was seeing it clearly.

"Oh!" I said, not able to restrain my excitement. "It's so beautiful." Then I covered my mouth to keep from saying anything more.

This was the Coat I had seen! This was the Coat that I loved—a glowing, white coat with gold braided trim. It flowed in soft pleats in a slim, straight line. Tentatively, I reached out to touch it. Just the feel of it made me laugh and cry with joy. It felt like cotton balls and cashmere, new babies' butts and small puppies' noses. It felt softer and sweeter than I had imagined.

Full of excitement, I ran down the stairs to where Rashana was waiting. "That's it!" I said. "That's the Coat I saw! I can't believe it! I'm so happy I could die of happiness right on the spot."

Rashana shook her head. "No chance of that," she said. "I'm not finished with you yet."

I looked up at the platform, and the Coat seemed radiant. "It's the perfect size for me," I said. "Can I try it on? I'm sure it will fit."

"Are you sure?" Rashana said. Then she hesitated before she asked, "Did you check the price tag?"

"I don't care what it costs," I said, trying to restrain myself while my own hands seemed to be clapping together without my volition. "It doesn't matter. I love it with all my heart. I have to have it no matter what. Can I try it on now?"

Rashana nodded and then lifted her hand to beckon the Coat forward on the platform. She took my hand and pulled me up the ramp. Up close again, the Coat took my breath away and made my heart beat as fast as it had the first time I saw it. I watched, holding my breath now, not daring to make a sound, as Rashana lifted it and began to place it on my shoulders.

"I know it will fit," I whispered, crossing my fingers.

But it didn't. I mean, it really didn't. Once it was on, I looked like an orphan child in an adult's coat. The sleeves hung to the floor, the shoulders were at my elbows, and it was so long that it draped like a Christmas tree skirt on the floor.

"Bring the mirror, please," Rashana called to EuphiU.

When I saw myself, I began to cry. "I was so sure it would fit," I said through my tears.

Rashana nodded. "I know," she said with sincerity. "But that wasn't the truth."

I tried to tuck up the sleeves, but made big lumps underneath the fabric. I tried to lift the hem off the floor, but my arms wouldn't go high enough. "I love this coat," I said again. "I want to be able to wear it."

Both Rashana and the EuphiU were staring at me but not volunteering any solutions.

I turned to EuphiU. "Couldn't you shorten the sleeves, take in some tucks, and stitch up the hem so it would fit me? Couldn't you alter it for me?"

Rashana grabbed her chest with both hands over her heart and fell backward in a dead faint. I heard a swish as she hit the floor.

EuphiU quickly knelt down alongside her, wings fluttering. I didn't know what had happened.

Finally after a little while, Rashana opened her eyes, and EuphiU helped her to her feet. She looked a little wobbly, but she managed to stand there long enough to say to me, with undisguised horror in her voice, "You want to *alter* the Coat of Truth?"

By then I had figured out it wasn't a good idea. "That's not possible, right?" I asked softly. "OK, I didn't know. I didn't understand. But you see, Rashana, I really want to wear it. So how else can I do that?"

Rashana turned to EuphiU and said in a despairing voice, "She hasn't learned anything! I swear I've worked with her constantly for lifetimes, and still there are some things she just can't grasp."

I got mad. "Don't talk about me like I'm not here," I told Rashana. "If you have something to say, then talk to me. Help me understand. I want that coat. Now, how do I get it to fit me? Just answer that one simple question."

Rashana sighed and then looked up toward the sky with a pleading expression.

It was twilight now. Watercolor pink and blue streaks and a few splashes of pale yellow crossed the night sky, making it look like a freshly painted canvas.

Rashana looked at me and said, "You have to grow into it, my little soul. Then it will fit. Then you can wear it."

"But how?" I protested. "How can I grow into it?"

She held up her fingers and pressed her forefinger toward her thumb and explained, "One small truth at a time. That's how you'll grow into it."

I couldn't stop the tears falling from my eyes, though I tried to hide them from Rashana as she took the Coat off my shoulders.

Before she handed it back to EuphiU, Rashana said to me, "You didn't check the price tag."

She held it out toward me.

It was hard to read, but through my tears, I saw it. "Price: More than you can imagine."

It was EuphiU who offered me advice and consolation. "It would have been much less disappointing and painful if you had chosen the Coat of Trust first. You should try to follow Rashana's suggestions. She truly is a bright spirit."

Chapter 8
The Coat of Trust

It was weeks before Rashana and I went back to the Yardsale, back to the Fashion Pavilion. It took that long before I could digest all that had happened. Finally, when I got over my hurt feelings and my disappointment, I decided to turn over a new leaf and try to cooperate with her more. So this time when she asked which Coat I wanted to see next, I told her I wanted to look at the Coat of Trust.

We sat on the bench in front of the Pavilion, and I watched and waited, trying to be patient, but nothing seemed to appear. Yet, at one point, Rashana exclaimed with excitement, "Nice, isn't it?"

"I don't see anything," I told her.

She frowned. "Look again," she said. "Look harder."

I looked again. The platform of the Pavilion was glittering silver, but it seemed cold and empty. I looked up to see if something was being brought forward on the Coat racks. I looked in the corner.

Then I shook my head. "I can't see anything," I said.

Suddenly, Rashana looked shocked. "Are you trying to see it with your eyes?" she asked.

I thought she was being a smart aleck. So I said, with condescension, "No, my dear little spirit. I'm looking through my mind's eye—through my third eye, if you will."

First she looked confused and then a little horrified, though to give her credit, she did try to hide it this time. She cleared her throat then and said softly, "Try to see it with your heart, please. The mind can only look; the heart can truly see. I should have given you better instructions. As a guide sometimes I forget the most basic but most important things." She looked sad for a moment.

"Don't worry about it," I said. "Nothing's lost."

She bit her bottom lip with her diamond-studded front tooth. "I hope not," she said.

I closed my eyes so I could see more clearly. I concentrated for several minutes. "I'm trying," I told her. "But nothing's happening. I still can't see that Coat."

"You can't try to see the Coat," she said a little too impatiently. Then she seemed thoughtful for a few moments before she said, "Excuse me. I've got to go somewhere for a moment. I'll be right back."

"Where are you going?" I asked.

"I need a second opinion," she said, "just to be sure I'm correct."

I waited for quite a while. At least it seemed like quite a while, and as I waited, I kept trying to see.

First I closed one eye and then another. I tried to see with my third eye, and then my mind's eye, and finally, through my heart's eye of Truth.

Oh God, I thought, shocked, when I saw the very faintest outline, the very faintest ghost of the Coat of Trust. It looked as though it was woven of cobwebs or lace, very delicate and fragile. It looked as though if a big wind came, it could be blown away or destroyed.

I was lost in thought when Rashana appeared by my side again. I was excited. "I think I saw it," I said to her. "The Coat of Trust. But it looks very delicate. I'd be afraid to try it on."

Again Rashana looked puzzled. "Afraid?" she asked. "What could happen?"

"I could tear it," I said.

She still looked puzzled. "So what?" she asked.

"Well, then it would be ruined," I said.

Rashana took a deep breath. She looked as though she had no idea where to begin. "You can't ruin that Coat," she explained. "You either put it on or you don't, and you can damage it, but once it's on, you can't ruin it."

I looked more closely. I'd never seen lace so fine. "It looks very delicate," I repeated. "What if I rip it?"

"It *has* to rip while you're putting it on," she explained, "or it wouldn't fit you."

"But then it would have a big hole in it, and I couldn't fix it," I said.

"The Coat of Trust grows as you grow," she explained. "When it rips, it repairs itself. That's part of its magic."

"Magic?" I asked.

Rashana tried to explain. "It's the first coat you wear as you come into the world. If you didn't already have one on, you couldn't have come to earth."

"I don't understand," I said. "Babies are born naked. They're not wearing anything."

Rashana shook her head. "When was the last time you looked at a baby? I mean, looked with your heart's eye of truth?"

"I hate to tell you this," I said, "but you're starting to sound like you're telling the story of the Emperor's new clothes. Only the children could see he wasn't wearing anything at all."

"Wrong," Rashana said. "That was the truth of the children of innocence. It's true that the Emperor wasn't wearing what the people were used to him wearing, but if you asked the wise woman sitting in the doorway of the hovel he passed in his parade, she could have told you that he was wearing the Coat of Trust. That coat is invisible to a lot of people but just because you can't see it doesn't mean it doesn't exist. It just means you can't find it if you're looking in the wrong place or looking with the wrong tools."

I looked again at the gazebo. I saw again that light, cobweb coat. "Who makes them?" I asked.

This time Rashana shook her head. This was one of those times I could tell she felt we weren't communicating. She looked up at me, smiled gently, and said, "Well, you see, there are millions of angels weaving them day and night. There's a big angel sweatshop in the sky where all those good angels work long hours for no pay out of their inherent goodness—"

"Stop, stop," I said, finally getting the joke. "Angels don't sew Trust Coats—even I know that."

"Right," she said, pleased. "Trust grows." She began to turn to go, but then turned back around and winked. "But in the angels' sweatshop, they do repairs."

"Get off it," I said, laughing. "Don't go just yet. I want to try it on and see how it feels."

Rashana looked at me hard. "OK," she said. "Climb up."

"Do you think it will fit?" I asked her as I walked over to the coat. "Or will I have to grow into this one, too?"

"It will fit," she said. "And it will grow as you do."

I reached out, and the coat seemed to float into my hand. It was completely weightless, so it was hard to manage because I couldn't always see it. But suddenly, as I began to drape it over my shoulders, I could feel it! I mean, really feel it. It was like a long, slow exhaling of a breath I'd held too long. I felt safe and warm and strong, as though nothing could hurt me. I began to spin around, feeling free as a bird and joyful. I began to laugh and laugh as I kept spinning.

Then I stopped dead in my tracks. I stopped spinning, stopped laughing, and stopped moving. I knew now that without this coat, I couldn't live any longer. But I had forgotten something. "Rashana," I said, still breathless from the spinning and laughing. "How much does it cost?"

Rashana smiled. "That coat will pay for itself."

"How?" I asked.

"I'm tired of explaining," she said then.

"But I don't understand," I told her as she started to walk away. "I thought everything in this Yardsale had been outgrown. I thought it was secondhand. Whose was this?"

"OK," she said, "let my try one more time. That coat is new. It's yours. It's a gift."

"From whom?" I asked.

"Grace," she said.

"Who's Grace?" I asked, and suddenly Rashana went into such a fit of laughter, she could hardly speak.

"Wear the Coat," she said. "It's yours. Trust me."

When we got to the gate again, Pete was waiting, polishing a silver watch. "Hi, Pete," Rashana said. "Beautiful moment, isn't it?"

"Sure is," Pete said. Then he turned toward me. "Nice Coat. Is it new?"

I just nodded, trying to understand. "It was a gift," I said.

"Always is," he said.

Then I asked him, "Still love toasters?"

Pete smiled. "Sure do," he said.

I stopped and knew I had to ask the question. "Pete, what's so special about toasters?"

Pete raised his eyebrows and then shrugged his shoulders. "Have you ever truly looked at a toaster?" he asked. He didn't wait for an answer when he added, "Every morning, I do. I look hard, and you know what? That toaster looks right back at me. Wears the same expression I do. The look in the eyes is the same. It reflects everything about me. And each toaster I look at, each moment in each day, shows me who I am. They're great, those toasters. Never lie to me. Show me who I am. Do just what they say they'll do. That's nice."

"Wow," was all I said.

"One day you'll see the great beauty in toasters," he said. "Trust me, you will."

I laughed. "I trust you," I said, because suddenly, everything he said made sense.

Chapter 9

The Coat of Change

It was the first day I'd ever been to the Yardsale when there were dark and menacing storm clouds overhead. Rashana was standing at the entrance waiting for me, wearing a bright-yellow raincoat; a big, brimmed rain hat; and matching rubber boots. She was carrying an umbrella made of stripped candy canes, and she was whistling a happy tune.

"I had no idea that it could rain at this Yardsale," I said to Rashana.

She looked puzzled. "Why?" she asked.

"I don't know," I said. "I just couldn't imagine it raining in the higher realms. I just thought the weather would always be sunny, and the days would always be perfect."

Rashana shook her head. "I don't get what you're saying. Are you saying that rain and storms aren't perfect? That only sunny days count?"

"Well, I guess in some unconscious thought or mind-set, maybe I did feel that way, but I truly wasn't aware of it," I explained.

"Tell it to those who are living in drought lands on your planet," she said, with a little edge. "Tell those farmers whose plants are dying that only sunny days count. Or those who are living in the desert lands with nothing to drink or eat."

"OK, OK," I said. "I was wrong. But there's no sense in making me feel bad because I imagined only sunny days as beautiful. That sounds like everything I heard as a kid—'Eat what's on your plate. You know how many starving kids there are in the world'?"

Rashana dropped her umbrella and pushed back her rain hat so she could really see me. "You never imagined a storm as being part of a perfect day, but you did imagine a spirit, or your higher self, or even an angel dressed in a raincoat, rain hat, and boots? I'm always amazed at how the human mind works!"

"Well, so there; we're even," I said. "I never imagined my higher self being like you. In fact, I have a question to ask, if you don't mind."

Now Rashana brightened right up. "At your service, Soulee," she said. "Ask away. But let's start walking before we get caught in the perfect storm."

I walked alongside her, just waiting for it to start raining or hailing or whatever it was going to do, and though nothing happened, those clouds seemed to follow us as we walked right into the center of the Yardsale to the Fashion Pavilion. "Where's Pete?" I asked. "I haven't seen him today."

Rashana smiled. "Probably running around covering all the tables in the Yardsale with rainbows in case it does rain."

"Nice," I said. "I love rainbows."

"Seldom appear on a perfect sunny day," she said, making a face.

Though we were now sitting on the white stone benches in front of the Fashion Pavilion, I didn't see the Uppity Angel anywhere around. I kept waiting for her to walk through the trestle, carrying another coat, but nothing was happening that I could see. So when I couldn't wait another minute, I said, "OK, Rashana, I know you're making a point, so why don't you just spit it out so I don't have to guess. I thought we were coming to see another Coat. What's going on?"

She looked at me and suddenly her raincoat, hat, and boots were gone, and she was wearing her fairy outfit and waving a magic wand. "I'm building a foundation," she said. "Or in mind thoughts, a strong premise, to rest my case on...or in this case, your next Coat on."

I sat quietly and murmured, "I won't even ask."

"Would you like to know something about the next Coat?" Rashana asked.

"Sure would," was all I said.

"OK, let's see if I can just give you an outline, and then when you see it, you'll be less surprised and maybe appreciate it more."

"You know the Coat I really like..." I reminded.

"Yes," she said. "The Coat of Truth. But there was an issue that had to be resolved first, right?"

I nodded. "Yes," I said. "It didn't fit. It couldn't be altered. And most importantly, I had to grow into it."

"Good job, Pumpernickel," Rashana said. "So let me give you some clues. The Coat of Change comes in *any* color—unlike the Dream Coat, which comes in *many* colors—and it's the Coat that you can wear through all your lifetimes. The Coat of Change can be light as a feather or heavy as leather, depending on your need at the time. It's sort of like an all-weather coat, and you change the lining to fit the situation."

I still couldn't picture it, so I asked her, "It has a lining?"

Rashana giggled. "That's what makes it so special. Different stories or narratives line this coat. There are adventure linings, and safety lining, and linings of purpose. It's the one Coat that you can keep wearing as you change and grow!"

I made a face. "I'm having a hard time picturing it. Can you keep describing it to get me closer? The way it sounds, it could be anything."

"Yes, yes," she said. "The Coat itself can be made for anyone, for it's a Coat made by Spirit, but your Coat is yours alone. Wait, wait, that's not exactly what I meant to say. I mean it's my Coat technically, not 'technicolorly,' but I give it to you as a soul when I think you're ready to wear it. And then it's your Coat alone until it's returned to me."

"Keep talking," I said. "Now it sounds like a Coat I'm going to have to borrow."

"That's OK," she said, smiling. "I don't mind. I made this one especially for you before this life at hand."

"You mean before I was born?" I asked. "Like beforehand?"

"Yes, just like I explained," Rashana said. "I considered the pattern before I considered you, with All in mind, of course. The lining is a narrative of your soul's journey, with changing scenes and characters. It's a new kind of fabric that stretches to match the growth of your soul. It's made up of an energetic, quark-like material—sometimes particles and sometimes waves—depending on their purpose and how much intention you can get into action. It has the ability and its own consciousness that enhances your life and changes as you do."

"Wait a minute," I said. "You mean you make the pattern, the narrative can make choices, and I get to wear it? Where does free will come into this? Mine, I mean?"

Rashana looked serious. She was thinking. "I get your point," she said. "I'd have to say it depends on where you live. How big is the closet that holds your Fate or Destiny? And how many shelves have you put aside to hold Free Will?"

"You just tossed me right off the cliff of my mind," I said. "There's no way I can even take a guess at that. Could you simplify? And stop using such big concepts, please."

I heard a chorus of music in the background, like a chorus of angels. Rashana didn't have a cellphone, but I knew "they" were trying to reach her.

She tilted her head to listen, and then she said simply, "It's a shapeshifter. You can morph in it. And when you wear it, you'll look just like what you want to be, and you'll be ready for wherever you want to go."

I swear, sometimes I need pictures to make things clearer, I thought. No sooner had I thought that then I saw the Uppity Angel walking under the trellis holding the biggest Coat I had ever seen. I gasped in surprise.

"You're kidding me," I said. "It's huge. It's way too big. It probably belonged to the Jolly Green Giant."

"Nope Soulee," Rashana said. "It was always ours. Want to try it on?"

I took a deep breath and then I said, "Sure, don't mind if I do."

When we walked up to the runway of the Pavilion, Uppity held the Coat up, and I slid it on. It was a beautiful lavender green, like no color I had ever seen on earth. And it was light as a feather and moved and stretched. It was covered with golds, silvers, and coppers with colored letters stitched into paragraphs and connected to other paragraphs. To my surprise, though it looked so immense, it fit me just right.

"How can that be?" I asked Rashana.

"Things are always changing, and you have too. You've lived a bigger life than you think you have, and you've finally begun to understand that change happens, always, all the time, to everyone. The bigger the experiences of pain and beauty, the larger the story. And so, we've built that coat to be big enough to fit—even with your ever-changing plans.

The Coat of Change had a thread of gold which wove itself through a constantly changing narrative in all kinds of fonts and letters. It was a Storyteller's Coat. Every experience I could remember—as well as some I couldn't—was already written in that coat. I could never have imagined a Coat like that, and to think it was mine was unbelievable. Gratitude washed over me like rain.

Rashana suddenly began to sparkle all over. She said, "So you can imagine it raining gratitude in your perfect world, but you can't imagine or appreciate the perfect storm?"

Suddenly the storm clouds above began raining crystal glitter confetti. "You made your point," I told her. "Don't be smug. It doesn't suit you."

"I love glitter, I love confetti, I love rain, I love the sun, I love the world, and I love you!" Rashana said, and she kissed me with great enthusiasm. "What a pretty purple, rainy-glitter day! You are my most perfect soul. I think I'm beginning to see the Light!

Chapter 10

The Coat of Love

Rashana and I were playing tag to pass the time, zigzagging across the yard in front of the Pavilion. I had gotten bored and wanted to go home again, but she insisted we weren't quite finished yet. I, on the other hand, was quite finished. I didn't want to see another coat after those I'd seen.

"You want your life to have meaning and purpose," she reminded me. "You asked for help. We visited the Angel Council, and everyone is behind us, offering us help, and now you want to quit?" She looked horrified.

"Don't say I want to quit like I haven't given it a good shot," I said. "I've tried on The Coat of Armor, The Dreamcoat, The Coat of Truth, and The Coat of Trust. I've even braved the Coat of Change. Now there's another Coat I'm probably not prepared for. A person can tolerate only so much 'knowing.'"

Rashana looked devastated. Suddenly, I knew what this was all about. I remembered something she asked me for early in our relationship. She told me that all she needed was one soul in one lifetime to reach freedom.

In a moment of weakness, I promised her that I would do all I could to help her get everything she needed to complete her grandest creation. It was a gift she'd been working on since her beginnings. And now it was almost finished; the beautiful rosy quartz necklace of all her soul lives. The only thing she needed to finish it was a golden clasp of pure love. Apparently, that was my part. She had asked, and I told her I would do all I could to help her. Though I thought it was really bad planning to take a soul who she'd placed in an enmeshed Italian family, send her to Catholic school, make her a nurse, and expect the outcome to be freedom. But she insisted she'd thought of that when she'd planned me. She thought we'd both enjoy the challenge.

"I so want a clasp," she repeated now, "for the necklace for the Lord."

I didn't give her a chance to finish cause I felt guilty. "How come you have an agenda?" I asked, annoyed. "I thought spirits were here to serve humanity."

"True," she said. "But what kind of a relationship would it be if it went only one way? I'm also learning and growing, and you're here to help me too. I may be smarter in the overall sense, but sometimes humans have a better feel for what earth needs. In that way, you help and teach me, so we both evolve."

I held my face and rubbed my eyes. "I didn't know that," I said. "I thought it worked differently."

"Like I do everything for you?" she asked. "That's it?"

"Don't make it sound so self-serving," I said.

"It is self-serving," Rashana said. "Even if we do things for each other, it's still self-serving. But what's wrong with that?"

"You wouldn't get it if I explained," I told her. "So let's just get this over with. We can go back to the Pavilion, and you can show me the next Coat. Okay?"

Rashana smiled and did a quick little zigzag step across the grass. She began to sing then, and her voice was like a gentle summer rain, sweet and comforting, "I want to be free, I want to be free..."

"Right!" I said, and laughed. "I want to be me..."

At the Pavilion, SI—the Spirit of Integration and EuphiU's left-hand girl—greeted us with a big smile. "Uppity is at the Council," she explained. "She's presenting a new creation to the Arcs."

"Arcs?" I said, confused.

"Archangels," Rashana whispered to me, and then she said to SI, "We'd like to see the next Coat."

"Of course," SI said. Then to me she said, "You must be really excited about this one."

I smiled. "Well, I'm never quite prepared," I admitted.

Si turned to go and suddenly on the Pavilion I saw this huge Coat that seemed familiar though it looked nothing like anything I had seen before. Except maybe one of those old traveling suitcases with the labels of where the people had been pasted all over. This Coat looked like it had really been around. But instead of labels, it had little patches that held complete scenes of different people, different locations, and different events.

Rashana looked way past thrilled with herself. "What do you feel?"

I looked at her and frowned. "What could I feel? It's crowded."

But that didn't seem to discourage her. "I helped design it myself," she said proudly. Then she added, "Of course you helped."

"Rashana," I said. "What Coat is this, and what are we talking about here?"

"The Coat of Love, my dear little soul," she said. "The next to the best Coat on earth." She took my hand then, and we began to walk closer so I could get a better look.

This Coat was embroidered with such intricate detail that I was amazed. Like an elegant patchwork quilt, I could see relationship patches, mother patches, lover patches, children patches, and friend patches. It was colorful and looked very resilient.

There were patches of me with my grandmother when I was just a baby, patches of me with my parents when I was young, and patches of when I got married and had my own babies. There were thousands of scenes from my life with all those I loved who loved me, and even some who didn't seem to. Yet they were all there, a testament in tapestry to the life I'd lived and the people I loved. The whole Coat was trimmed with gold braid.

"Wow!" was all I could say.

"'Wow'?" Rashana said, making a very unangel-like face. "A lifetime's worth of patches, and that's all you can say? 'Wow'?"

"Well, I'm sort of speechless," I told her.

"OK, let me tell you the greatest thing about this coat," she said, and then she reached for the hem and pulled one of the strings, and another whole row of patches fell down, lengthening the Coat even more.

"Oh," I said. "Let me see those pictures."

Rashana shook her head. "How can you see them when you haven't lived or loved those scenes yet? They're waiting to be embroidered in, but they can't be—until you live them. You see, my dear Timid Soul, some of those you love you haven't even met yet. Some of the places you'll go you haven't even dreamed of yet. The Coat of Love, you see, is a coat that is always being altered. In fact, when a soul is born, it's only a short jacket. It takes living and loving to grow it. It takes experience."

"Well," I said, smiling happily now, "it is colorful, and it looks interesting. Like it would be lots of fun. Can I try it on?"

Rashana hesitated for only a moment before she explained, "This Coat is reversible, Soulee. The outside of the Coat is the love you give, and the inside is lined with the love you get." And then she mumbled something I couldn't hear.

"I'd like to try it on," I told her again.

For a moment she looked as though she wanted to say something, but then she seemed to change her mind. Instead she walked closer to the Coat, took it off its heavenly hanger, and held it up so I could slide into it.

"It looks so big," I said, remembering how disappointed I was when I'd tried on the Coat of Truth. But when I got this Coat on, it fit perfectly, as though it was made for me. I spun around once and then twice and asked her, "How does it look?"

"It looks wonderful to me," she said. "How does it feel?"

Suddenly, it felt like someone had left a label on that was scratching me behind the neck, making me very uncomfortable. "What's this?" I asked, reaching for it.

Rashana walked up and began to study the patch.

"Not outside," I said. "It's the inside that bothers me."

"I know," she said. "I was just checking out which one it was. It's the time right after your grandmother died. Your family had gone to the funeral, and you were home sitting on the stoop—"

"I'm asking about what's bothering me about the Coat," I interrupted. "I remember the scene."

"It's the inside lining," she explained. "Every one of these patches has a lining. Some are smooth and soft, some are rougher, and some have thorns. I forgot to tell you: the Coat of Love is multisensory. It's filled with all the emotions you had at the time you experienced the relationships. It will take a while, but you'll learn how to achieve the best experience when you wear it."

"Ouch," I said. Just then something stuck me in the butt. "What was that?" I asked.

"Your divorce," she said.

"Say no more," I told her and began to take the Coat off, but she stopped me. So I asked her, "What happens if I turn this coat inside out and wear the outside on the inside?"

"Good idea," Rashana said. "Then the love you've given will be the closest to you, and it will feel much more comfortable."

"Funny," I told her. "I always thought The Coat of Love would be prissy and filled with little hearts and cupids with arrows. Something warm and fluffy, not something with itchy labels and thorns."

"That would feel rich," she said, smiling at me mischievously. "That would be a real experience of love on earth."

"Don't be a smartass if I ask a dumb question," I said. "I just have to know. What is this Coat for—I mean, aside from recording the loves of my life, which we could also do with a photo album or a digital CD?"

"Duh," she said. "What kind of question is that? Would you rather wear the Coat of Fear?"

"Wait, wait, wait," I said. "Who knew those were the only two choices?"

"I did," she said. "Most other spirits who know anything at all know it too. I mean, unless they were born yesterday."

"So that's why it's so valuable?" I asked.

"Well, one can't wear the Coat of Love and the Coat of Fear at the same time, so it's actually a Coat of Protection from Illusion. That's the truth of Love."

"Wow," I said again.

"Stop with the 'wow,'" Rashana said. "You really have no idea how 'wow' this coat is. In fact, it's the next-to-last Coat you wear on Earth, and then when you slip out of this one and into the next, this coat goes to the Universal warehouse so that the karmic scribes can archive it with the rest of our lives."

"They don't have computers to scan it?" I asked.

Rashana wore a puzzled expression. "Of course we have computers that scan. But not to file important judgments like the weight of your heart against the weight of a feather. Those kinds of determinations need a personal touch. Only the Higher Ups in the Hall of Judgment can do that."

"Let's not go there," I said.

"We can't go there now," she said. "But we will have to someday."

"Next Coat?" I asked. "Bring it on."

"Can't do that," she said. "It's in the warehouse on layaway, and I don't have the ticket. Only the All holds that. Only the Creator knows when it will be picked up. Until I get the call, no Coat."

Chapter 11

The Radiant Coat of Death

When we walked away from the Fashion Pavilion, even though I had tried on the Coat of Love and really felt good in it, I was sulking because I didn't get to see the last Coat. I wanted to finish this lesson on Coats.

"What Coat is it?" I asked. "The one that I don't get to see?" I tried to remember what was left.

"One of the most beautiful Coats on Earth," she said dreamily. "It's the Radiant Coat of Death. Although that name itself is a misnomer. Here we call it the Coat of Grand Transitions. Once you put that on, you'll really know what freedom is."

"You make it sound like a Concord flight," I said. "Like it breaks through all the barriers of sound and light."

"Yes," she said. "That captures the concept better than the word 'Death.' Your word 'Death' sounds like it's a destination instead of a rest spot. But human livings come to many 'conclusions' before they go on to their next steps." She smiled then. "So now you have it. All of it."

"I can't really wrap my head around where I'm going when I stop living," I admitted. "I mean, I know you go on—but what about me?"

Rashana took my hand. "Well, you and I will be closer than ever," she said. "Once you get through the Recycling Center."

"You're kidding, right?" I said. "You just made that up."

"No, I didn't," Rashana protested. "It was made up long before even I was made up. How it goes is, God gives breath, and God—or the Source—takes it away. Then we wind up really close and go to the R&R&R&R&R in the recycling center, where first we have the Review, followed by the Reward, then the Reintegration, the Renewal, and finally the Radiance."

"Sounds cool," I said. "What happens after the Radiance?"

Rashana shrugged. "We decide where we want to go and what we want to experience next. That's it."

"All of it?" I asked. "There are no more Coats?"

"Only one left in this line," she said. "The Coat of All."

"What's that like?" I asked.

"Well, as I recall," she said, laughing, "it's no Coat at All. For it's only on Earth that there are separations. Everywhere else, All is One."

Chapter 12

The Wrap

Rashana and I were walking toward the Gate, and I was feeling very satisfied. I had tried on all the Coats I could, and there had been no unpleasant surprises. I was excited to tell Pete about them.

Now I turned to Rashana, but she was doing cartwheels in a large circle behind me. "Hey," I shouted. "Angel mine, so that's it for now, right? We're done with all the Coats of Meaning. We're finished. No more Coats."

Rashana put the brakes on her cartwheels and within a deep breath she was standing right next to me again. "What did you say?" she asked.

"I said we're done. There are no more Coats, right?"

She rubbed her hands over her eyes and then down over her face until her fingers were over her lips. Then she looked me straight in the eye and asked, "Does it *feel* to you like there are no more Coats?"

"Oh, don't get all therapeutic-sounding on me." I said. "It makes you sound insincere."

"I'm just telling you the truth," she said. "Does it feel finished to you?"

"Well, I did wonder why there was no Coat of Beauty or Coat of Freedom," I admitted.

Rashana let out her breath with relief and didn't even wait for me to finish. "Of course there's the Coat of Beauty and the Coat of Freedom. There's also the Coat of Wonder, the Coat of Abundance, the Coat of Empathy, the Coat of Service, the Coat of Purpose, the Coat of Transformation, and, of course, the Coat of One, which is one size fits All. But it's really All Size Fits One, with lots of elastic or stretch quarks."

"Then why did you call it the 'Eight Coats of Meaning' if there are so many more?" I asked her. "Why did you say only eight?"

She was offhanded when she said, "Well, those eight are like your basic black. All the rest can be layered." She smiled, very pleased with herself. "You've already outgrown the Shadow Coats of Fear and Arrogance. The Coat of the Cross or Suffering was so worn out it was threadbare. And others have been outgrown or discarded, like The Coat of Separateness which is sometimes called the Boundary Coat, and it was one you refused to wear."

I frowned, trying to process what she had said. When she saw my expression, her eyes twinkled, and she giggled. "I didn't tell you about the Robes either. The Coats are individual constructs for NOW, but the Robes are leadership constructs and need a longer commitment. There's The Robe of the Hero, The Robe of the Goddess, The Robe of the Mother...."

Now I held my hand up to stop her. "Don't! No more," I said. "Not now. I'm overwhelmed. It's like too much info. A soul can only grasp so much at once."

Suddenly Rashana looked at me with intensity. "I forgot," she said compassionately. "I get so joyful when I'm able to share the gifts for faster-growing evolution that I forget." Then she reached into her pocket and handed me a marshmallow. I popped it into my mouth. "This is soft, easily chewed and digested," she said, smiling. "A marshmallow a day!"

I was still chewing when I said, "That's not how it goes. It's an apple a day keeps the doctor away."

She shook her head. "I don't agree," she said. "Sleeping Beauty made that mistake when she took a bite, and look at what happened to Eve." She giggled again and asked, "Isn't it funny how people make things up?"

We were close enough to the front gate to see Pete, so I asked Rashana, "Well, what happens next?"

"I thought maybe we could go to the Godspeak Concert," she said. "Do you like music?"

"I do," I said. "But I've never heard of Godspeak. Is it a new group?"

"No," she said. "It's been around forever."

"Can I think about it? I asked. "I mean, before we go on a whole new adventure, can I just take a break and spend some time in ordinary consciousness?"

"Sure," she said, smiling. "Let me know how it works out for you."

The End

There's an Angel in my Computer
by Carol Gino

This is the Quest for a Divine vision and the ways in which prayers are answered. Carol Gino offers her journey with amazing honesty and hope and shows us the ways in which each of us can open new pathways to communicate with our own inner guidance.

This wise and witty dialog explores both path and purpose and shows us a space in which the human soul can touch the heart of God.

Available at: http://www.aahabooks.com
Also available as an ebook!
Search for this title at your favorite eBook seller.

Visit aaha! Books: http://aahabooks.com
for books, audio and more products by Carol Gino

email: team@aahabooks.com
Carol's Websites:
http://carolgino.com
http://aahabooks.com
http://rashanasgarden.com
http://hopefulhealer.com

Facebook Pages:
https://www.facebook.com/carolginoauthor
https://www.facebook.com/AngelinmyComputer
https://www.facebook.com/GuardianAngelCircle
https://www.facebook.com/thehopefulhealer

Facebook Group:
https://www.facebook.com/groups/Nurseswhocare/

Twitter:
https://twitter.com/Hopefulhealer

YouTube Channels:
https://www.youtube.com/user/Carolgino
https://www.youtube.com/user/NurseBytes
https://www.youtube.com/user/RevolutionaryNurse

www.ingramcontent.com/pod-product-compliance
Lightning Source LLC
Chambersburg PA
CBHW022039170626
46808CB00003B/1283